A Salisbury Tendresse

and other tales

A Salisbury Tendresse
and other tales

RADU HERKLOTS

Copyright © 2024 Radu Herklots

The moral right of the author has been asserted.

Apart from any fair dealing for the purposes of research or private study, or criticism or review, as permitted under the Copyright, Designs and Patents Act 1988, this publication may only be reproduced, stored or transmitted, in any form or by any means, with the prior permission in writing of the publishers, or in the case of reprographic reproduction in accordance with the terms of licences issued by the Copyright Licensing Agency. Enquiries concerning reproduction outside those terms should be sent to the publishers.

This is a work of fiction. Names, characters, businesses, places, events and incidents are either the products of the author's imagination or used in a fictitious manner. Any resemblance to actual persons, living or dead, or actual events is purely coincidental.

Troubador Publishing Ltd
Unit E2 Airfield Business Park,
Harrison Road, Market Harborough,
Leicestershire LE16 7UL
Tel: 0116 279 2299
Email: books@troubador.co.uk
Web: www.troubador.co.uk

ISBN 978 1 83628 016 3

British Library Cataloguing in Publication Data.
A catalogue record for this book is available from the British Library.

Printed and bound in Great Britain by 4edge Limited
Typeset in 11pt Minion Pro by Troubador Publishing Ltd, Leicester, UK

Foreword

Writing these stories has been a labour of love. I hope that my loyal crime-fiction readership will forgive this change of direction, but to ease the temporary transition I have included a bonus story which features John Tedesco, Barker and the familiar Rhyminster cast. They will be back next year.

Choosing the order in which to place the stories has been quite difficult. I imagine that this is how recording artists feel when arranging songs on an album.

Do I start with the title track? Or is there an obvious hit single that should go first? Do I finish with the up-tempo bangers, or with a quiet one?

I hope that once you start reading, you persevere as I am sure there is something for everyone.

All the stories are set in places where I have lived, worked, or have spent significant time, so there is a natural bias towards the counties of the southwest.

A word about 'Awaiting'. The idea for the artist, Edmund, was inspired by the imagined early life of Devon artist RJ Lloyd, who was perhaps best known as the illustrator for some of Ted Hughes' poetry collections.

I am fortunate beyond words to have inherited two of

his works, one of which, *Lych Gate at Hartland, 1968* is the template for the prized picture featured in the story.

I must also mention Dr Jennifer Nias, who died in 2023 after a long life dedicated to primary education. Lucinda and I spent countless happy weekends and summer holidays at her house in Cornwall, and one of the stories is set nearby.

Jenny was my most rigorous critic, so I hope she would have approved.

And finally, thank you to Adrian Crick for giving me permission to quote from his beautiful poem *Autumn Men*, and to Lucinda; this one's for you.

Contents

Graham's Trip Home	1
Backwoodsmen	6
Stephen and Joanna: A Salisbury Tendresse	9
Maureen the Community Champion	34
The Cowardly Groom	43
Awaiting	56
The Price of Love	68
The Autumn Men	74
The Comeback	88
A Cornishman's Imagined Journey Home for the Final Christmas	96
A Close Encounter: John Tedesco Investigates	98
About the Author	113

Graham's Trip Home

He was dreading it, that final visit.

Graham had held it together at his father's funeral; glad-handed the punters, gracefully accepting their shy condolences.

"We are so sorry for your loss."

"He was such a lovely guy."

And from the vicar: "Try and be kind to yourself."

Graham, the eldest, had been born at home. There had been complications with the birth of his sister, Julie, and so she came into the world at the old hospital, Freedom Fields.

Mum and Dad had lived in the little house in Saltash Passage for over half a century, bravely starting married life in the aftermath of the War as the shiny new city of Plymouth emerged, as if by magic, from the dreadful bombing that had all but destroyed the old centre.

Graham still had hazy memories of going with Mum to see the opening of the new Tamar Road Bridge in the lee of Brunel's masterpiece.

Mum had said that it was 'modern'. Everything had been 'modern' or from 'up London' to her. He missed her so much.

Graham had, according to family legend, been way more

impressed with the mayor's mighty chain of office than he had been with the appearance of the Queen Mother.

He didn't recall that, but he did remember the space-age toll booths, which seemed like something out of *Doctor Who*.

Julie escaped to Southampton University as soon as she had left Devonport High for Girls, armed with good A levels, ambition to burn and a grim determination never to move back.

Then it was on to London and a career in the media. She rarely came home after making her escape, and the visits all but dried up once Mike and the kids arrived.

The last few months had put a huge strain on her big brother.

He had also moved away from home, but only got as far as Dartmouth, where he worked as a draughtsman for Bazeley's, an architectural practice with a good local reputation.

He'd have loved to have got married and had children, but it never happened.

"Too nice," the girls at the office used to say.

"Poor old Graham. He's so good at dealing with his dad and all the admin," everyone said. "But it's not as if he has anyone else to look after," they would add.

They didn't mean to be unkind.

He'd gone down there every week after Mum had passed, whatever the weather, and he would drop everything, including, he sometimes felt, his own prospects for career advancement or personal happiness, if there was an emergency.

He'd been the one who sorted out all of the scam calls; the one who broke it to Dad that his driving days were over. He'd been the one who had witnessed the slow decline, and the narrowing of horizons.

Dad didn't want to have Sunday lunch at the garden centre anymore. He had even lost interest in the fortunes of Plymouth Argyle Football Club, a sure sign that he was tuning out.

Although Graham lived in the same county as Dad, the drive to his old home could be slow and tiring, especially if he came down after work.

He started to dread turning into the little unadopted lane and finding that there was no parking space available, and then he would suffer his weekly agonising wait after he rang the doorbell before Dad's dark shadow eventually hove into view.

On this last visit home, the heart-sinking feeling was replaced by the sensation of dropping feet first into a bottomless well of sadness.

The house had sold quickly in the mad Covid rush to the southwest, for way over the asking price.

"More money than sense, boy," he could imagine Dad saying.

Graham became a regular at the Chelson Meadow Recycling Centre – the tip – and he used up half his annual leave in clearing the house.

Julie had shown little to no interest in assisting and, lacking her brother's sentimental nature, didn't want any souvenirs.

So, Graham endured the lonely task of deciding what to chuck out, becoming gradually more ruthless as he went through the countless albums of family photos.

He got a bit for Dad's medals and his collection of Argyle programmes going back to the 1950s, but the time soon came when he had to abandon the remainder of the contents to the tender ministrations of the clearance guys.

And now, here he was, drawing up outside the house for the last time.

He tried to tell himself that it was just bricks and mortar, but it was so much more, wasn't it?

A loving home where two special people had set out into an uncertain but exciting future, and where two lucky children had grown up in the security of a village community, but thrillingly close to the shining new city by the sea.

As he got out of the car, Graham noticed straightaway that the estate agent's sale board had been removed. It had been unceremoniously dumped in front of the garage.

There was a skip beside the house, and the air was full of the aroma of sugar soap and primer.

Despite remembering that he had agreed to the buyer's request to have access to the garage for storing some furniture, he was still somewhat taken aback to find that the decorators were in.

A young woman came running down the stairs at the sound of Graham unlocking the front door. "You must be Mr Brimacombe," she said anxiously. "I'm sorry for your loss," she quickly added. She let Graham in and offered him a tea or coffee, which he politely declined.

He said, "I'm just calling in to check that all's well before I hand all the keys to the agents for completion tomorrow – but I see that you have already started!"

She replied hesitantly, "Oh, yeah, do you mind? I know we are only supposed to be storing stuff, but as the house is empty…"

Graham took it all in his stride. If they wanted to start decorating, then it probably didn't matter. What could go wrong now – it was only one day when all was said and done.

The woman asked if he wanted a final look round, and so he climbed the stairs to his old bedroom for the last time, the walls long denuded of his old Thunderbirds posters. But his heart wasn't really in it, so he went back downstairs and made to leave.

As he did so, the woman's partner – a burly bloke with visible tattoos on his neck – was lugging a huge television over the threshold.

He put the TV down and Graham introduced himself. "Mr Brimacombe! Yeah! Nice one! Sorry for your loss," said the bloke.

As he exited the front door, Graham noticed that his father's roses were coming out.

"Dad loved his roses," he said out loud, to nobody in particular.

"Aw, bless," the woman said, her partner adding that he wasn't a gardener and so he thought they might replace the lawn with astroturf.

Graham took this as his cue to leave and drove round to the estate agents to hand over the remaining keys to the property.

Once he'd done this, he walked back up the street, crossed the road, found a spot where he could look across the river to Cornwall and then he stood there motionless and waited for the tears to come.

Backwoodsmen

Friday night in the Carpenters Arms. No sign of the cost-of-living crisis here, nor any serious observance of dry January.

The major and his cronies were occupying their regular positions on the rickety bar stools, the gamekeeper and his latest conquest were warming their ample backsides by the fire and the members of the PTA executive committee were enjoying their monthly social by taking full advantage of the chance to snipe at the headmistress behind her back.

Mine hosts Bill and Jackie were away enjoying some winter sun in Cape Verde, only too happy to leave the staff in charge for a week or so.

The conversational buzz was suddenly interrupted when the major ostentatiously tapped his personal tankard on the counter, calling for silence at the bar.

"I'm going to have to whisper this, in case the Woke Police are listening in."

"I don't blame you," said Mike the electrician, adding that he had been fitting some outside lights for a 'new' couple just in time for Christmas and she, 'the bird', took offence at him for using sexist language. "Christ, it was only a bit of harmless banter."

"Anyway, as I was saying," the major went on, with more than a little irritation. "The PC brigade have gone too far this time," he continued. "You remember my little scheme to extend at the back, open up the views over the Quantocks?" He knowingly paused for effect, like a government minister addressing the faithful at the party conference. "This little shit from the council, a limp-wristed idiot called Wakerley, called round to the house this afternoon. 'Ooh, Major Prendergast,' he said. 'I have to inform you that we have received multiple objections from owners of neighbouring properties focusing on your proposal to create a vista by removing protected trees from the site.'"

If the major was expecting sympathy from his audience, then he wasn't to be disappointed. A mass outbreak of head nodding and tutting ensued.

"I reminded him how long my family have lived in this village, the impertinent twerp, and then I challenged him to name any of these objectors."

Barry the thatcher butted in. "I can give you their names, Major. Mr D Duck and Mr M Mouse!"

This brought the house down, the mirthless laughter bouncing off the old beams of the ancient tavern.

"I bet it was those tree-hugging Greens again," said the gamekeeper.

"And the climate activists," Barry added.

"Or bloody Remain voters," offered the gamekeeper's companion.

"My round, I think," boomed the major, who ordered in several pints of Retribution, the local ale.

The grandfather clock in the snug was just making its leisurely way round to half-past eight, which was the last time for food orders, when an effortlessly elegant couple strolled in and confidently took the small table in the corner.

They looked like they had just landed from another planet. He was wearing a club blazer over a crisp white shirt, with a navy-blue silk tie and matching pocket square, and she looked stunning in a dazzling scarlet trouser suit with matching heels.

But it wasn't just their clothes that made them stand out. They were the only black people in the pub that night.

The man walked up to the bar with a practised confidence, and ordered two glasses of the house red.

"Shiraz or Merlot?" asked Amelia, Bill and Jackie's daughter and occasional stand-in bartender.

An eerie, rather nasty silence descended over the bar, punctuated by some urgent whispering as the man squeezed past the regulars and then carefully transported the drinks back to the little table.

"Down from London, you reckon?"

"Never seen the likes of them in here before. What sort of man drinks wine in a pub?"

Once they had finished their drinks, the woman stood up and, having correctly identified the major as the leader of this group, she walked up to him, looked him firmly in the eye, and offered her hand.

"Good evening. My name is Clare Stevens, and as of an hour ago, I am your Conservative candidate for this constituency. I do hope that I can count on your support."

The major stood open-mouthed as the candidate turned to her husband, and then the pair of them glided silently out into the night.

Stephen and Joanna: A Salisbury Tendresse

Stephen

As a rule, I've never been one for recalling dreams, but every rule has its exception, and I recalled this one. And I acted on it.

It was a very insistent dream, as if it was telling me to jolly well make sure that I remembered it this time.

It was remarkably simple. There wasn't much of a plot.

You see, I just felt myself being gradually guided by the beam of an enormous lighthouse, but as I got closer, I could tell that it wasn't a lighthouse after all. It was more like a large pointy spire with a light on the top.

I have lived a quiet life. I am single, have become reconciled to it, but I am no stranger to unrequited love. It would be a bit odd if I wasn't, seeing that I'm nearly sixty.

My shyness is the problem. Never been able to get past it.

I'm a teacher in Kingston upon Thames – maths. I think I must be quite good as I get asked by some of the pushy parents to give extra tuition. They offer to pay me.

It is a lot of money, but I never agree. Why should these

kids get priority over the others? They already have a head start.

So, I prefer to help the strugglers, and I hold special classes for them in my own time.

Home is a nice little place in East Molesey. I can get the bus to work, and there is a train to Waterloo from Hampton Court, although it is very slow. On Saturdays I might go up to London if there is an interesting film at the iMax, or I sometimes queue at the National for the cheap tickets. I always go to the afternoon shows, as you can't rely on the last train home.

I can only afford to rent my house. The landlord is a former teacher at the school, whose wife inherited a fortune. They used it to invest in the buy-to-let market and it seems that they have done very well. They have been very kind to me. They haven't put the rent up for a long time. I am a model tenant, apparently.

Anyway, my real passion is walking. I've tried out various ramblers' groups over the years, but I prefer to head out on my own. It isn't just the shyness. I like to be alone with my thoughts. I find it peaceful to be in the middle of nature. Kingston is very nice, but it has become more crowded since I started work in the 1980s.

I always feel better after a long walk. 'Good for your mental health' is what people say these days.

But there are downsides to walking on your own.

I went down to the riverside in Richmond the other evening. It was lovely – one of those never-ending sunsets over the water. I decided to stop and take in the view.

Let me explain. I went to an exhibition of paintings of the Thames at the Courtauld Institute last year, and there was one by an eighteenth-century artist called Marlow, which he had painted from near to where I was standing. That was why I had decided to go to Richmond – so I could locate the precise spot where the artist would have stood.

As I turned and walked on, a young girl, probably in her twenties, difficult to tell these days, was walking towards me.

She opened her mouth and said, "Fuck off, pervert."

I was horrified. Why would she do that? It must be awful for women to feel that all men are beasts like those metropolitan police officers.

I felt like going back and trying to speak to her. "Not all men are like that," I would have said. "I am no threat to women, or to anyone actually. I'm not very brave but I have called out a racist."

This was true. I am quite proud of this. One of my walking tours in the Easter holidays had been on a section of the southwest coast path, going by stages from Weymouth, along the Jurassic Coast and ending up in East Devon.

I had booked to stay in a farmhouse bed and breakfast on the Devon/Dorset border. It had been a hard day, lots of steep climbing and walking along sections of pebbly beach.

The man who ran the place was watching television in the reception area when I arrived with my rucksack, tired out. It was the late 1980s, and Trevor MacDonald was reading the news.

"I'm always interested in the opinions of the young," said the man. "So, my son, how do you feel about having our national news read out to us by a darkie?"

I told him that I wanted to cancel my booking as I didn't want to stay with a racist. The horrible man kept my deposit, but that wasn't the issue. I just wanted to get right away from him and his vile views. I couldn't believe that there were still people like that.

I picked up my rucksack and struggled on to Seaton, where I managed to find a room in a pub. It was alright.

So, back to my dream. I've gone off at a tangent, haven't I?

Just thought I'd throw in a little maths reference…

Coming right up to date, I booked a weekend's walking along somewhere called the Clarendon Way, which is an ancient pilgrims' route between Winchester and Salisbury.

I caught the train to Winchester after work on the Friday and had a good wander around after I had checked into a very nice bed and breakfast near Winchester College.

I was very impressed with the buildings. I don't suppose that the 'Wykehamists' – which the nice lady who ran the establishment told me is the name for people who go to the college – had their maths lessons in portacabins like my students.

The lady, who was called Emily, asked me if I wanted an early breakfast as I had told her that I was planning on walking the Clarendon Way when I booked the room.

The weather was a bit drizzly as I set off after my excellent fry-up, but I didn't mind. Better that than hiking in a heatwave.

There were a few walkers around, but none of them seemed to be going the whole way. A number of them had dogs with them.

I have often thought about getting a dog. I might not feel like such an outsider if I had a dog with me. Perhaps the poor girl who swore at me might not have done so if I had a little border terrier by my side, or a Jack Russell perhaps.

I might have to revisit this idea.

The Clarendon way was turning out to be a lovely walk, not as challenging as the southwest coast path. I think it will make it into my top ten!

I stopped and ate my lunch by the River Test, which was beautifully clear, and then I continued to a place called Kings Somborne, where I had booked a room at the village pub.

A chap at the bar tried to engage me in conversation. I was enjoying a pint of the local beer – I think it was brewed near Alresford – when he started to chat.

I tried to battle the shyness, but he wanted to talk about the football results, and I don't know anything about football. I don't really like it, which I know makes it hard for men like me to fit in, especially in places like pubs.

I slept quite well, and the next morning I ate something called a 'Hampshire breakfast', although I wasn't clear about what was particularly 'Hampshire' about it. It just seemed like a standard fry-up to me.

After a grey morning's walking, the sun came out in the afternoon and as I looked ahead, I could see the spire of Salisbury Cathedral in the far distance. All I could see was the spire.

It looked like it was sprouting out of the fields. I couldn't see the cathedral itself until I reached the last part of the walk.

After a hot and sweaty descent into the town, I decided to find some tea before I caught the train back to London, and as I wanted to see the cathedral as well, I tried the refectory, which was still open. The roof was made of glass, and you could see the spire through it. The tea was very welcome, I can tell you.

I have never been someone who has revelations really. It's probably the maths teacher in me. But I think I had one that day as I was travelling on the train home.

I realised that it was Salisbury Cathedral that was beckoning me in that dream. It wasn't a lighthouse. They are meant to warn. The cathedral was welcoming me, as if it was pointing the way to the next part of my life.

Joanna

It was the news that I had always dreaded. Dad could no longer manage on his own.

Since Mum died, he had slowed down to barely walking pace. Like a lot of men I have known, he has always been rubbish at friendship, never keeping up with his old mates from school, university, or the hospital, so he had no real support network after his beloved wife died, and he would have rejected any offers of help from his friends even if he had made any conscious effort to keep in touch with them.

And he would never have sought out new groups. He is the last person I could imagine in a Men's Shed repairing old bikes, still less taking up walking rugby or bowls.

I should have told you – Dad studied sociology at the LSE and then came a series of management roles in the NHS, finishing up as chief executive at Salisbury District Hospital.

Mum was a linguist. They met at university, and she taught in the various places where he was posted. She found it easy to get jobs because:

There always seemed to be a shortage of language specialists.

She was a superb teacher.

Everyone loved her from the moment they met her.

She made my dad, in so many ways. She gave him the

confidence to apply for senior positions, and she organised their social life. Their houses were always happy places, with people popping in, frequent dinner parties and their legendary Christmas cocktail evenings.

I think I am quite shy, and so I take after Dad in that respect, but I am not sure that is how I come across as I hide it really well.

I look more like Mum though, with my jet-black hair and hazel eyes. One of my old boyfriends from way back in the day used to tell me that I looked a bit like Linda Ronstadt. I'd take that.

At this stage, I need to point out that there was a family tragedy which blighted our lives, which may have contributed to my shyness. But writing this, and seeing it on the page, I can tell that it might read like a glib excuse.

My baby brother Jeremy was born with a weak heart and died suddenly when he was only three.

It hit us all, but Mum rallied Dad and I, and told us that we all had to carry on for Jerry. And with a hell of a lot of bumps on the way, that is what the three of us did.

Now that I am putting this down on paper, I wonder whether Jerry's death affected me in a subtly different way. I had rebelled against by parents by insisting from quite a young age that I wasn't going to waste three years of my life by going to university.

We have all met people who boast that they are the first person in their family to go to university; I boasted that I was the first in mine not to do so.

So, I wonder if the tragedy subconsciously led me to the conclusion that life was short, so let's get out there, earn some money and get on with it.

Get on with it is what I did.

After my A levels I spent a year at secretarial college, and soon found an evening job in a local restaurant, so by staying at home for an extra year instead of following my friends to 'uni', as nobody called it back then, I was able to build up some savings.

"It's never too late to apply, darling," Mum said. "You got three As! Why don't you just treat this as deferring for a year?"

No way. As soon as I'd finished the course, I took myself and my certificates from the secretarial college to Nottingham Railway Station and jumped aboard the first train south to London.

I'd already found a room in a house share in Shepherd's Bush and spent that late summer applying for jobs.

So, there I was, by mid-September, setting out on the life I had dreamed of. I began in a typing pool in the City, swiftly moving up the ranks to become the well-paid PA to one of the directors, finding myself a place of my own to rent in Belsize Park – you could afford to in those far-off days.

I had fun as well, but never found anyone to settle down with, not, if I am being honest, that I wanted to.

Through tuning into the market gossip from my work, I became a shrewd small investor, and built up what I called my 'Sod-Off' fund, which I could use to escape if I got tired of the job.

Of course, Mum and Dad worried, and couldn't understand why I hadn't settled down with a nice young man. And they were getting broody. They wanted grandchildren.

There were two things that I could have said to them, but didn't:

The only nice man I was ever serious about was neither young nor single.

How could two LSE graduates from the sixties become so numbingly conformist?

Then, after fifteen years of living life on the slipstream of the fast lane, I began to realise that I was getting bored with the world of finance. I had turned down the chance to move upwards, more than once, partly as it involved exams, but mainly because it would mean working even more crazy hours.

I had no one else to provide for, and I had picked up a couple of cheap student houses at auction back in Nottingham that I could rely on to supplement my generous pension from the private bank.

I could also feel how the wind was blowing. Secretarial jobs, even at my stellar level, were becoming redundant.

Bizarrely, it was on a rare trip to see my parents – I could kill two birds with one stone by checking on the buy-to-lets at the same time – that I happened to mention to Dad that I was looking for a change of direction.

He knew a Harley Street consultant who saw private patients in Nottingham once a month. Dr Fernandes had mentioned to him that he needed someone to manage his practice, as the old trout who had been his secretary for decades was getting past it, and he'd gently persuaded her that now was the time to retire to Sidmouth and spend more time with her hymn writing.

The interview, if you could call it that, took place over a long lunch in Rules, and the charming Dr F asked me to name my salary, which I did.

The bank made polite attempts to persuade me to

continue with them, but my old boss took me aside and quietly told me that I'd made a shrewd move.

So, until the sober realisation hit home that Dad needed me with him, my life revolved around managing the practice of a famous doctor and his demanding patients. I absolutely loved it.

I spent just shy of fifteen years with my employer, and had become indispensable to Dr F, so I was flattered, but not surprised, when he made a big effort at persuading me to stay. As I said, I loved the work, and was immensely proud of the trust that he had placed in me, and so it was only ever going to be family duty that could tempt me away.

The doctor and I tried to make it work part time, but it soon became clear that I couldn't just rely on the carers.

My father kept escaping, going walkabout, and as the errant daughter I was guilt-tripped into mercy dashes by the neighbours.

He was finally referred to the memory clinic by his GP, which resulted in a diagnosis of vascular dementia.

The last straw came while I was dealing with one of our 'household name' patients – that dates me, they call them 'celebs' these days – when I was interrupted by an urgent call from Salisbury.

The morning carer had found Dad on the floor. He'd been there all night, and he seemed to have forgotten how to activate the alarm on his wrist.

The woman had called for an ambulance, but she couldn't stay with him for long as she had other clients to see.

"But I am in London! And I'm *incredibly* busy!" I yelled at her, unable to conceal the exasperation from my voice.

I got on the phone and managed to persuade one of the

neighbours, a prickly pear called Ursula, to sit with him until the ambulance arrived, her passive aggression making it clear that she felt that it was my duty to sort this out.

He'd had a mild stroke, which, apparently, can be related to his diagnosis. Who knew?

So, I very reluctantly handed in my resignation, and moved down to Wiltshire to look after him.

Without any siblings to share the burden, I was soon struggling despite the carers, who were lovely with Dad, even though he couldn't distinguish between them.

He called them 'My nice tubby ladies'.

When I did manage to escape from the house for my weekly treat of a trip to Waitrose – Salisbury was turning out to be quite civilised – I would think selfish, unforgiveable thoughts as I dithered at the wine section.

I had moved away from my parents as soon as I could; it was a conscious decision. I never asked for this. I never signed a contract agreeing to be responsible for them in their old age. Or was there an obligation smuggled away somewhere in the small print of the terms and conditions of life?

Then I'd go back and take over from the afternoon tubby lady and spend the rest of the evening soaking in a cold bath of self-loathing. I've pleased myself all my adult life, and here I am whining about having to accept *some* responsibility.

Really, after I think about all they did for me. I truly am an ungrateful cow.

I busied myself by gradually tidying and improving the house, buying in 'new-fangled' kit like a dishwasher. Dad was always a late adopter when it came to gadgets or technology. His philosophy was to stick with the old until it became impossible or rude not to. And he actually enjoyed washing up.

I wonder if it gave him time to himself, listening to Radio Three while he went at it with the Marigolds and the Fairy Liquid.

I sorted out his broadband and bought him a modern TV, as his had the smallest screen imaginable, the guy at the dump asking if he could keep it as it was 'a retro classic'.

So, while I couldn't pretend to be living the dream, I did reach an accommodation with the situation, and I kept in the back of my mind the reassuring thought that it couldn't last for ever.

Dad still recognised me, thank the Lord, and frequently told me how grateful he was that I was doing all his paperwork. Mum had bullied him into making out a Lasting Power of Attorney. Well done, Mum!

After a while, the tubby ladies all agreed that he was fading, and I finally had to admit to myself that they were right. The last thing to go was his politeness, and his closing words to me reflected that innate quality.

"Thank you for being a wonderful daughter."

Looking back, I have come to terms with his passing. I no longer feel so guilty, as I was there for those precious last months, and it really was a privilege.

If I can allow myself a tiny pat on the back, I am sure that my being there kept him out of hospital. And if the spectre of guilt appears at my shoulder, as it still does sometimes, I can scare it away by pointing out that no one will be there to look after me when the time comes.

Stephen

As I write this down, I still can't quite believe it. After all my years of quiet inertia, I have become quite the man of action.

Inspired and convinced in equal measure by my revelation, I confided in David Parker. He was my best friend in the staff room. We used to go to the Spring Grove for a pint or two of Young's IPA after work on Fridays to put the world to rights, or to decompress, as he would put it.

David taught economics, and I relied on him for advice on money matters.

I had begun to worry about my retirement since my mid-forties. I was lucky enough to have had a couple of small inheritances, but I still fretted about being able to afford to buy something in the area where I lived. Renting was all very well when I was working, but I craved some security in my old age. I think that is fairly normal.

David had advised me to put most of my savings into stocks and shares ISAs, and to hold the balance in cash.

I wasn't sure at first, and I have always been wary about the stock market because it struck me as a form of gambling, but David's advice has paid off.

I had started to look up property prices online, and when I confided in David, he said he would go through the figures with me; while he was pretty sure that southwest London would be a stretch, I should be able to find something suitable in Salisbury.

And I did. I spent several days down there in the Easter holidays, which convinced me that my revelation must be acted upon.

Everyone I met seemed to be so kind, even the estate agents. I looked at several properties and kept in touch with

David Parker. He told me to avoid leasehold or anything that would need too much work.

Then, just as I was losing confidence, I found exactly what I wanted. It was a nice little terrace in a suburb called Harnham, near the river but walkable into town. There was even a pub nearby overlooking the water.

David came down on the train for the day to accompany me on the second viewing, and he was very firm.

"This is a gem, Stephen. Don't mess about in this market. You are a cash buyer, so make them an asking-price offer in return for a period of exclusivity."

I am so lucky to have someone like David in my corner.

The next day, he texted me what I think was a joke: *#straightouttaharnham!*

It's going to be my new hashtag, apparently.

Then, before I knew it, Natalie the estate agent called to say that my offer had been accepted.

Time began to move quickly. I arranged a survey, which was largely reassuring, and there was no chain holding things up, so I was able to move during the summer holidays.

The headmaster was very understanding when I told him that I was retiring and said how I had been one of the best teachers he had ever worked with. Wow.

I was given a lovely send off, and a very generous cheque from my colleagues.

When I arrived to take my last-ever class, I saw that someone had chalked the words 'Sir is a legend' on the board. I found that very moving.

So here I am, in sunny Salisbury, surrounded by packing cases, ready for a new start. And who knows, I might even find that special someone.

Joanna

Organising the funeral was surprisingly time-consuming, although Dad had left detailed instructions for me.

The funeral director was obsequious to the point of being slimy, reminding me of one of those creepy gentlemen's outfitters on that comedy sketch show from thirty or so years ago.

Having resisted his slithery attempts to sell me the platinum package, I asked him to arrange a fairly basic funeral at the local church in Harnham, followed by a wake in the church hall.

Over fifty people turned up, which was about double what I had expected. Mainly his surviving ex-colleagues, but there was the usual unexpected relative, in this case a crushingly boring cousin from Daventry who wanted to tell me about his complicated car journey, clearly confusing me for someone who might be in the least bit interested.

The worst part was the evening afterwards; letting myself in to what had, until recently, been my parents' home, pouring myself a large gin and tonic and suddenly realising that I was alone, an orphan, with no one in the world.

I have never really experienced yearning and have never had a problem with finding intimacy when I needed it, but I am starting to wonder if I might be ready, after all this time, for a steady relationship. That's what losing both parents does, perhaps.

Although I would never have expected it, caring for Dad seemed to have given me a new purpose in life and a different perspective.

Maybe I should do some voluntary work, bringing home-made soup or calf's foot jelly, whatever that is, to the sick, or start shaking a collection tin at the train station?

I certainly had decisions to make – where to live for starters. Dad's place was too big and gloomy for me, so I resolved to get it on the market asap.

But I quite liked Salisbury. I didn't really know it until I gave up work to look after Dad.

On my rare visits to my parents after Dad got the chief executive job, it tended to be an overnight stay, and we rarely ventured out of the house.

The town – technically a city due to the huge cathedral – had a lot going for it.

It boasted a theatre and an Everyman Cinema; there were plenty of other concert venues, and it was well connected by rail, so I could keep in touch with my old life. And the natives were spookily friendly.

Anyway, I was able to buy myself some time by selling the Harnham barn, as I had come to know Mum and Dad's place, which went amazingly quickly and for way more than the asking price, and then renting myself a flat in the old training college in the Cathedral Close.

The income from the Nottingham buy-to-lets more than covered the rent, and I was sitting on the proceeds from the house sale, so I was completely financially independent.

My temporary abode was quite basic, and most of my neighbours were ancient, but I soon began to relish my surroundings. It felt so secure being locked in behind the wall in the Close every night. This was the original gated community after all.

I am in no way religious, but even I couldn't live opposite a gothic wonder and never peek inside. I decided to have a look around on a busy Saturday morning when there were hordes of tourists, as I was less likely to be approached by some goofy canon wanting to talk about Jesus than if I had wandered in on a gloom-laden wet Tuesday afternoon in February.

Although I was shocked to be asked to pay to enter, I was reassured somewhat by the fact that I could use my ticket for the rest of the year. A bit like a McDonald's bottomless coffee, perhaps?

Anyway, despite my instinctive hostility to religion and churches, I was stunned by my first sight of the interior, the massive gothic arches, and the incredible view from west to east, uninterrupted by any pesky screening.

I turned down the chance to be guided by some old crone wearing a green sash who looked for the world as if she was an air stewardess on a Dignitas flight, but as I mooched around quietly on my own, I found myself listening in to what the guides were saying.

It sounded fascinating, but I felt that they could do with some younger volunteers who could more easily relate to twenty-first-century tourists.

Now that I have been a guide for a few months – how crazy is that! – I cannot believe how wrong I was. That old crone has become one of my best friends. She is called Virginia. She is a whiz at IT, goes on Extinction Rebellion marches and prefers Tom Jones and Neil Diamond to choral music.

And far from being creepy and wanting to sell me God, the cathedral clergy are refreshingly down to earth and normal. Who knew, eh?

I wear my green sash, and I wear it with pride.

Stephen

After a slow start, I gradually got used to the rhythm of my new home city. David came down for a few days to help me settle in and I have discovered some lovely walks from my front door.

I was walking along the Town Path one bright sunny morning when I saw a sign that read 'Public Drownings This Saturday'.

That certainly got my attention. I knew that I had moved to a medieval place, but this seemed a little extreme. Upon closer inspection, the poster was advertising a demonstration of the flooding of the water meadows to raise awareness of the work of the Water Meadows Trust.

I went along that Saturday, and I must say that it was a fascinating and, as it turned out, life-changing experience.

A large crowd had gathered, and two experts wearing bowler hats, the drowners, explained about the history of the water meadows and the way that water was captured and then released to irrigate the land.

They opened one of the sluice gates and the water gushed out like a tsunami. I made sure that I got some good photos of that!

Anyway, after the interesting demonstration there was coffee and a cake sale in a tent, and I fell into conversation – gosh, haven't I changed since moving here – with a very nice lady called Virginia.

I explained to her that I was new to the area, and she said that if I was looking for something to try, why not qualify as a cathedral guide?

This is what she had done after her husband died, and

it had given her a new lease of life, meeting visitors from all around the world as well as her fellow volunteers.

"You need to train, of course, but you are in luck – the next course starts in a couple of weeks' time."

She texted me the details, and I decided to give it a go. It was going to be held every Saturday for six weeks and, in the meantime, there will be the opportunity for some on-the-job learning with one of the 'teams' as they are called.

I was put in the Tuesday morning team. Having been one of the oldest teachers at the school, I found that I was one of the youngsters in this group. They were all very welcoming, and I got to know them during the tea breaks between the guided tours. Many of them had been quite important before they stopped working. There were retired army officers, doctors, and, to my pleasant surprise, a good number of fellow teachers.

The course was very well structured, but it was quite hard work. We were given a book of facts about the cathedral which we had to learn. Some people dropped out if it wasn't for them, but I stuck at it.

We all had to take a turn at explaining something in the cathedral, such as a memorial, or the font, and then we were marked – or critiqued as they say nowadays.

I talked about one of the stained-glass windows which was inspired by prisoners of conscience and was thrilled to be told that I had good presentation skills. I can explain equations, of course, but I didn't know if I would be any good at talking about windows!

There was a woman on the course who was very striking. She was younger than most of the trainee guides, and probably a few years younger than me.

She was always very well turned out, even if she was dressed casually. I noticed that she wasn't wearing a wedding ring. I am not the kind of man who normally notices things like that, but I have to confess that I was quite pleased, relieved even, by the lack of a ring on her finger.

I tried to talk to her during the lunch break, but she was deep in conversation with the tutors, and I didn't want to interrupt.

Of course, not wearing a ring didn't mean that she wasn't in a relationship, but there was something about her that made me determined to try and get to know her a little. I hoped that she would be in the Tuesday group, but she wasn't.

I could ask the head guide which group she was in, but I think that might be a bit, you know, stalkerish. Which I am most certainly not.

I'm sure our paths will cross at some stage. I have learnt that the locals refer to Salisbury as 'Smallsbury' because you keep bumping into the same people in the market and round the town – sorry – city!

It is just a matter of time.

Joanna

I am really enjoying it here and have started looking for a house to buy. I can't afford the Close, unless I get another flat, but there are some promising areas nearby with good views, and I can move quickly.

My social life has taken off. I have joined a group of guides who go to the theatre. It is amazing to have somewhere like the Playhouse on the doorstep, and the group sometimes ventures further afield to Bath and Southampton, which are both easy to get to on the train.

To my pleasant surprise, I seem to have acquired a number of admirers around the cathedral, including the Bishop's chaplain, who must be twenty years my junior.

He's quite dishy, but I think I would soon wear him out. Be a good scandal while it lasted though, but I might get drummed out of the guides, and that would be a shame.

And I've grown out of toy boys. Probably.

There is someone. I noticed him on the guides' course. He seemed a bit lost, but he had a kind face, as Mum would have said. I clocked him checking out the ring finger of my left hand and he blushed like a teenager.

Virginia, who knows everything, has found out that he's called Stephen, and that he's taken early retirement from teaching. He's in the Tuesday morning group and they all think he's lovely.

Stephen clearly isn't the type to make a move, way too shy, and probably a representative of that dying breed, the true English gentleman. So, I will have to make it look as if he has – made the first move, that is.

This will require care, as I expect that he scares easily.

I wonder if he's going to the volunteers party at the Deanery?

Stephen

I still haven't bumped into the striking lady from the guides' course, but I have accepted an invitation to the volunteers party. They hold it every year. It is the cathedral's way of saying thank you for all the hard work that the guides do, as well as the stewards and all the other groups.

I wasn't going to accept, as I am a newbie and don't feel

that I have done enough hard work yet, but my colleagues in the Tuesday group have rather insisted that I come.

I am hoping that she will be there, of course, but even if she doesn't turn up, it will be fascinating to see inside the Deanery.

The dean makes it her business to talk to the volunteers. She came into the refectory and had tea with a group of us the other day.

She hasn't been long in post herself, but she knows Salisbury as she grew up nearby on the coast in Dorset, so she says that she has returned to her roots. She loves sailing and has a boat on the River Hamble which is just outside the diocese of Salisbury. I expect that she likes to be anonymous when she can.

I really am pleased that I moved down here – I wouldn't be hobnobbing with people like the dean if I'd stayed in East Molesey!

Stephen and Joanna

Dean Gillian was enjoying hosting her first volunteers' party. If she was being honest, she had been dreading it, but the guests were on their best behaviour.

They had done all the catering themselves, and the organising committee had even offered to stay behind and clear up.

Her predecessor had warned her that the volunteers could be a tricky bunch, forever falling out with each other over all manner of trivialities and imagined slights, but that hadn't been her experience thus far.

She was impressed by the sheer wealth of life experience

in the room, and by how positive these mainly elderly crew members were about the cathedral.

Excusing herself from a brewing debate about the best way to showcase the Magna Carta, she approached one of the younger guides, probably in his late fifties or early sixties, who she had remembered from her last foray into the refectory. Nice man.

Scanning the room as she crossed the floor, she noticed Joanna, who was clearly trying to extricate herself from a conversation with one of the adult choristers.

It wasn't difficult to notice Joanna. She wasn't conventionally pretty, but she had something, more than a flake of stardust.

"Joanna! I was hoping to run into you. I hope Hugo isn't monopolising you! There is someone I'd like you to meet…"

***

Joanna was the shy one that evening, and Stephen later wondered if he had been too garrulous. "I've messed up again, haven't I," he told the mirror when he got home.

But, upon parting, they had agreed to meet at evensong the following Friday night, and as kindly autumn made its annual pirouette towards the harshness of winter, this became a regular highlight of their week.

These meetings were good first dates, if that is what they were, as they didn't have to say too much to each other, they could just let the glorious music flow over them.

And, although Joanna's icy hostility to organised religion was still in its slow thaw, it helped that the evening service demanded nothing of its congregation.

After a while they decided to have a Sunday lunch together at the Yew Tree, a cosy village pub a few minutes' drive from the Close.

Neither of them could remember who suggested it, nor what had caused their fingertips to brush together for an electric nanosecond as they discussed the payment of the bill.

They split it equally and left a good tip. They were both well brought up.

A fortnight later they went to a talk over in Winchester about William Walker, the diver who saved that cathedral from sinking, then Stephen started to go on the theatre visits, and as they gradually got to know each other, they began to recognise the loneliness and pain that they had, in their different ways, been made to go through in order to approach this delicate tipping point.

Virginia and her friends in the guiding community thought that Stephen and Joanna would make a lovely couple, and that perhaps the guides should give fate a helping hand or at least a gentle nudge by encouraging this nascent romance. Could there be wedding bells?

But Stephen and Joanna had other ideas. They seemed to have reached a happy place. They had become very special to each other, more than friends but not quite lovers. A Salisbury tendresse.

***

A tendresse does, by implication, allow for tender moments. As they walked across the frosted cathedral green together after the magical candlelit advent service, a first for both of them, they faced each other and shyly and, of course, tenderly, kissed goodnight under a huge tree, just as the moon was paying a passing visit.

Cue choirs of angels rejoicing.

Maureen the Community Champion

"So, Mrs Lugg," said Michelle, "it's your big day. Let's get you looking your best for the mayor, shall we?"

"Just the usual, nothing fancy," Maureen tartly replied to her hairdresser.

Michelle and her colleagues referred to themselves as stylists, but they were only hairdressers so far as Mrs Lugg was concerned.

What is wrong with people these days? she wondered to herself, *giving themselves all these airs and graces.*

She was 'Mrs Lugg' to all but the chosen, hand-picked few upon whom she was prepared to confer the great honour of calling her Maureen.

Never Mo or Renie, oh no.

Mrs Lugg had recently been nominated for an award in recognition of her years of voluntary service to the community.

For many years she had been a stalwart of, amongst others, the horticultural society, the ladies' bowls team, and St Andrews Church, where she had steadfastly served in all the major offices of state: head flower arranger, coffee-rota supremo and churchwarden.

"I bet you are excited," said Michelle, risking a daringly novel opening gambit in comparison with her ritual enquiry about holiday plans.

"Excited? No, not really. I think they should just stamp my forehead with the word 'MUG' on it. When I think about what I've given over all this time, and for what? A pat on the back from that idiot."

"Do you mean the mayor?"

"Little Trevor Shepherd? I remember him from when he was a lad. Used to try and take stuff from the shop. Now look at him."

Mrs Lugg and her late husband Arnold had owned the town of Bullercombe's only newsagent and tobacconists. A *high-class* newsagent and tobacconists.

It was a Spar now, and Mrs Lugg had never ventured across the threshold, preferring to rely on Asda's home-delivery service rather than encountering the pot mess that the new people had doubtless made of her once-pristine shop.

After Michelle had finished faffing about with the mirror, Mrs Lugg pronounced herself satisfied – not happy, mind – with her shampoo and set.

The stylist, knowing better than to expect a tip from this very particular customer, followed her to the door.

"Bye, Mrs Lugg. I will expect photos!" said Michelle, with a futile attempt at jollity.

There were three recipients of awards at the town hall that afternoon. The lollipop lady, the cheerful old boy who sold poppies for Remembrance every year and, the last to be presented, Mrs Maureen Joyce Lugg.

Trevor Shepherd, the mayor, read out a citation that described her as an unsung hero.

At least they got that bit right, she thought to herself, before she was shuffled off to the mayor's parlour for the official photographs.

"It's that drooling old lecher from *The Times* again," she muttered to herself as the elderly photographer took an age to arrange the group shots.

"Come on, Mrs Lugg! Smile!"

She grimaced, then she did allow herself a smile, more of a smirk really, but not for the photographer. She was fondly remembering the days when holidaymakers from up country ventured into the shop during the summer to buy their daily papers.

If they asked for *The Times*, Arnold would deliberately present them with a copy of the *East Devon Times*.

"Oh, it was the *London Times* you wanted! Why didn't you say? We don't get much call for it down here."

Arnold would be spinning in his grave if he saw the town now. It was artisan this, craft that. Nothing for normal folk.

The tea rooms had, inevitably, become 'Suki Braine at Number Seven'.

She was another one down from London. She'd finished second on some cooking show and wanted to come down here and take advantage of the wonderful local produce. She was certainly taking advantage.

Mrs Lugg had seen an article about Ms Braine in her magazine.

You would need to be missing a few brain cells to pay her prices, assuming you could afford them in the first place, she thought to herself, reflecting that what the town could do with is a decent bus service and a proper baker, not all this organic nonsense.

Lockdown hadn't helped the local economy of Bullercombe, although Mrs Lugg had quite enjoyed the initial experience. The weather was nice, the locals had the place back to themselves and, once she could meet up outside with Yvonne and Eunice, she had all the socialising she needed. Why did the peace and tranquillity have to end?

It was the post-lockdown period that brought all the trouble. Gangs of yobs from all over the country getting drunk, ranting, and raving, and the wild campers in the fields leaving litter and even raw sewage in their wake.

"Bring back National Service!" Arnold would have said. And he would have been right, as ever.

An elderly widow now, she was too frightened to venture outside for fear of being approached by these louts. Mrs Lugg was almost – only almost, mind – missing the normal tourists, for all their condescending ways.

And then all these people from up the line suddenly decided to move down here, pushing up the house prices and clogging the lanes with their huge tank-like vehicles, being clueless on what to do if they encountered a combine harvester coming in the other direction.

Talking about 'down from Londons', Mrs Lugg and her allies, Yvonne and Eunice, had a shiny new target for their vituperative comments.

No AI computer programme could have designed a more perfect hate figure for them than Sally Ann Juniper. Her very name was designed to wind up the locals.

It was bad enough having to put up with a woman vicar at St Andrews, Reverend Clare with the purple hair. Not a patch on Father Hatherley. He was one of their own, born and bred in the town.

But Sally Ann Juniper! She had enraged Maureen and her coven in the following ways:

Her husband was nowhere to be seen. He worked in London and travelled abroad a great deal – or so she said!

She lived in a huge barn conversion which could have housed several local families.

Her revolting children made a noise in church. Mrs Lugg would prefer it if children didn't attend until they were at least eighteen.

She wore a leather mini skirt to the bring-and-buy.

She existed.

This was by no means an exhaustive list.

***

Scrolling forward a few months, La Juniper had ingratiated and then integrated herself into Bullercombe life to the extent that she was directing the Christmas panto, had put herself forward for election to the parish council and, in her ultimate triumph over Maureen, she was now in charge of the flower arranging at St Andrews.

Mrs Lugg called a council of war, and on the following Friday evening, she, Yvonne and Eunice established base camp at Yvonne's picture-postcard cottage just off Fore Street.

The three widows decided that the time for radical action was overdue. Oh yes, things had gone too far.

Yvonne had been helping out at the Christmas bazaar when she overheard Sally Ann Juniper talking loudly on her mobile phone, presumably to one of her London friends.

"You must come and visit, it's so beautiful. Your room awaits!"

Then there was a gap while Sally Ann's friend babbled away before Yvonne, with the benefit of decades of experience at eavesdropping, caught the priceless gem: "What are the locals like?"

"Narrow-minded, clumsily conspiratorial. In a word, ghastly!"

***

Yvonne's late husband, Peter, had been the town gunsmith. The shop was used as a 'yoga and meditation centre' now.

His widow thought that this perfectly summed up everything that was wrong about the world today.

Eunice and Robert, on the other hand, had both been teachers in Exeter. Neither had taken any nonsense inside or outside the classroom. Never, ever.

They were a conservative couple with a fundamentalist approach to their Christian faith. Eunice had stopped going to St Andrews when Rev Clare arrived, because they couldn't accept the idea of a woman priest.

"So," opened Yvonne, "what are we going to do about Mrs Juniper? I've still got keys to the gun safe."

Maureen and Eunice seemed to be mulling this over, weighing up whether, on balance, a summary execution might just be a tad harsh in this case. Tricky one.

"Hmm," murmured Eunice. "Perhaps we need to be more subtle. How about some anonymous letters to the local paper? Or an online campaign?"

Maureen, who hated the very mention of 'digital' or 'online', had already concocted a plan, which she now shared with her fellow conspirators.

"Sad Sally will be at the carol service, won't she?" she began, receiving nods of eager agreement from the others.

***

Her sisters in subterfuge readily approved her brilliant scheme, which was carried out to perfection on the night.

Maureen had from time immemorial organised the welcome desk for the festive singalong, which, apart from a couple of lessons from the Bible and a watery address from Rev Clare, was basically what it was. And yet it still, inexplicably, attracted a large crowd.

This year she would make absolutely sure that Sally Ann Juniper would be rostered on duty with her.

The lady volunteers always left their coats and handbags in the vestry so that they weren't incumbered while performing their vital tasks, and Maureen knew that Sally Ann would bring her huge designer bag with her, as it seemed to be surgically attached to her shoulder.

Once the carol singing was underway, Eunice, who hadn't relaxed her boycott of services at St Andrews, would nip into the vestry via a side entrance. If it was locked, then she could use the spare key that Yvonne had got cut for her at the locksmiths in Honiton.

Maureen, meanwhile, had smuggled out some unused Gift-Aid envelopes from the church. These were used for the collection by those who still insisted on making their offering in cash.

The gang of elderly desperadoes then carefully placed various small amounts of money into these envelopes before sealing them tight. Yvonne printed the names of various regular worshippers on the front of the envelopes as well as some made up names of visitors in order to identify the 'donors'.

The 'donations' totalled fifty-five pounds, but the three of them agreed that this would be money well spent.

Come the night of the carol service, Eunice, wearing gloves, approached the side door during the lusty singing of 'Hark the Herald', and managed to enter undetected without needing the key.

She quickly located the ostentatious handbag, which she expertly unzipped before stuffing it with the gift-aid envelopes and then she swiftly hid the bag under an umbrella stand before stealthily departing the scene, her work done.

Meanwhile, Maureen held her nerve until the end of the service, when she joined the other volunteers as they trooped into the vestry with their bulging collection bags and baskets.

"My basket seems a lot lighter than it should be," she said in earshot of as many people as possible.

"Where's my handbag! It's very expensive, and it's got my phone in it!" shouted a clearly distressed Sally Ann Juniper.

Then, to coincide with the arrival of Reverend Clare, Yvonne applied the coup de grâce.

"Is this your bag, Mrs Juniper?"

"You know it is. Give it to me at once."

"Not before I have a look inside," said Yvonne, who unzipped the bag with a theatrical flourish, causing the envelopes to flutter to the stone floor with a certain parachute-like quality.

"I thought my basket was light," Maureen said, not quite succeeding in supressing a sneer.

***

It was the best Christmas that Maureen had experienced since Arnold passed away.

The church council agreed not to press charges, despite this being a crime of gross dishonesty, on the basis that Sally Ann Juniper agreed to resign forthwith from all her voluntary roles in the church and the town.

The newcomer had been so looking forward to her first beautifully curated Christmas in Devon with her family and her carefully chosen guests, but instead she had to spend it quietly with her in-laws in Buckinghamshire, from where she continued to protest her innocence.

But that was that in so far as country living was concerned for the Junipers. The monster barn conversion went on the market in January, and they resolved to move back to the Home Counties at the earliest opportunity.

As for Sally's nemeses, they were already hatching plans for the New Year. Following the success of their opening mission, Suki Braine was next on their hit list, followed by the artisan baker and the craft brewer.

Yvonne produced detailed plans for assassination attempts on the presenters of *Escape to the Country* and *Countryfile* but after due and careful consideration, she was outvoted.

Maureen, Eunice and Yvonne recognised that it might take them a while longer to dislodge Reverend Clare with the purple hair, but they were working on it.

The Cowardly Groom

Benedict blamed his best man. What on earth had Rob been thinking about? He was supposed to be looking after him. That was what best men were for.

He'd assumed that the guys would have got any silliness out of their systems during the stag weekend in Sofia – after all, two of them had ended up in hospital – but now here he was, puking his guts out in the early hours of his wedding day.

After desperately guzzling water as if he had suddenly discovered an oasis in the Gobi Desert, the bridegroom decided to go for a walk to at least try and start the process of clearing his head.

"You stupid, stupid idiot," he muttered to himself as he struggled into a clean pair of jeans.

Rob and Gavin had persuaded him that it would be in his best interests to come out for a quiet pint yesterday evening to calm his nerves before the big day.

Benedict had readily agreed, as he really had been pretty anxious.

His mother-in-law to be, the redoubtable Fran, was getting her knickers in a twist about the seating plan, and his own parents, who had decided to drive down from

Hampshire on the big day, as Lyme Regis was only a couple of hours away, had been constantly texting him, his mother extracting a solemn promise to have a nice early night.

He should have listened to her. If only he had.

Of course, it had turned into a pub crawl. After the 'quiet pint' at the Volunteer, they wobbled down the hill to the seafront, stopping at the Royal Lion for a 'quick one' on the way, before visiting the Royal Standard and the Harbour Inn, ending the evening in the Cobb Arms.

He didn't remember by what miraculous intervention they got back to the flat above the Old Post Office that Rob had hired for the weekend, but the key point was that they made it back before he was tied to the harbour wall or chucked into a fishing boat, or worse.

Wrestling with the laces of his trainers, he reassured himself that there was no danger of disturbing the others – they were snoring for England – so he carefully negotiated the stairs and exited the large Victorian building by way of the communal entrance.

Stumbling drunkenly into the day, he saw that white vans were making their early morning deliveries, but apart from them, and a solitary jogger, he had the town to himself.

In different circumstances, he would have relished this early start, walking through the deserted narrow lanes off Broad Street leading down to the mill, or enjoying a bracing stroll along the Cobb as the sun came up.

But as he headed down Marine Parade in a futile search for a takeaway coffee, he was hating every minute. All he could focus on was getting over the hangover from hell before the ceremony, which would be held in the Alexandra's wedding chapel at 2pm, and keeping away from Gav and Rob.

As soon as they surfaced, they would be diagnosing a fry-up – 'breakfast of legends!' – followed by more beers.

And he still hadn't told her.

***

The 'away team', as the best man had with precisely zero charm designated the bride and her family, were by total contrast enjoying an idyllic start to their day.

They were staying at the Alexandra, and the weather was kind enough for them to enjoy breakfast on the terrace, which gave onto a beautiful lawned garden overlooking the sparkling sea.

As announced to the readership of the *Daily Telegraph*, Sophie was the eldest daughter of Commander Andrew and Mrs Frances Ward of Bosham, West Sussex.

The younger daughter and chief bridesmaid was called Emily. To the commander's unspoken regret, there was no son.

Mrs Ward's angst over the seating plan had apparently gone with the dawning, and so she and her daughters were anticipating a calming pre-wedding build-up of spa treatments and pampering before the visit of the hairdresser.

The commander had, of course, commandeered one of the local fishermen to take him out for a spot of mackerel fishing.

While the old sea dog was heading off to the harbour, there were the first signs of stirrings from the remaining occupants of the flat over the Post Office. As Gavin groaned and grunted on his way to the kitchen, he stopped to knock on Benedict's door.

"Oi, last morning of freedom, you old w*****!"

After receiving no response to his increasingly loud hammering, he carefully nudged the door open, before waking up the best man.

"Rob! He's done a runner!"

***

Benedict had escaped, but only as far as St Michael's Church, less than one hundred yards from the sea, but nicely tucked away from the main tourist areas.

He wasn't really sure what had led him there, apart from the fact that it was open at that time of the morning, and he would be by himself unless some curious tourists wandered in. He certainly wasn't religious, and wouldn't have the first idea how to pray, but somehow the absolute quietness he felt in this place, as if he was wearing his noise-cancelling headphones, allowed him some welcome thinking space.

He and Sophie had been together for three years. He worried why she wasn't more surprised, taken aback even, by his sudden proposal, but it turned out that she had been waiting for it since they first met.

His parents loved her, and his dad had even told him that he had been playing a risky game by leaving it so long. No pressure then.

Everyone was happy. He was making everyone happy. But he wasn't happy because he still hadn't told her.

He wandered around the church and was briefly distracted by the window commemorating Mary Anning, the local woman who began digging for fossils in the early nineteenth century and who achieved fame when she found the first ichthyosaurus on the site when she was ten years old.

There is a statue to her on the seafront now, and a film with Kate Winslet.

Benedict wondered whether Mary Anning would have wanted to be portrayed in a film starring Kate Winslet or anyone else for that matter.

At that moment, he was very definitely craving anonymity but swiftly realised that going the full Greta Garbo wasn't going to work on his wedding day.

The shops were open now, so he could buy a can of cola and sit on the beach until the hangover started to recede, then he would lumber back up the hill to the flat, have a long hot shower and prepare for the dreaded ceremony.

He couldn't tell her today. He'd wait until they were on the Amalfi Coast.

***

The rhythmic sound of the waves gently rocked him into a natural sleep, but this was short-lived as he was awoken by the approach of Gavin, his expensive-looking trainers beating out a staccato pattern on the sand as if it was the skin of a drum.

Gavin slyly kicked the groom in the ribs, then bent over and yelled in his ear.

"Wake up, you lazy sod! Rob's sent out a search party."

Benedict came to, and after a couple of foal-like attempts, he managed to stand up again.

Gavin glared at him. "What were you thinking? We all thought you'd had second thoughts."

"Who else knows about this? Not the commander. Please not him. And definitely not Frantic Fran…"

"Calm down, I was winding you up. It's just me and Rob. Fancy a fry-up followed by a few beers?"

"What's the time? Oh no, I'm meeting the folks in ten minutes!"

This was a white lie. Benedict's kind, unworldly parents Cliff and Heather were still over an hour away.

"Look, I'd better leg it back to the place and get my act together. Why don't you two go and find something to eat, and then we'll meet up at about one – should allow us enough time to get togged up."

So, Benedict was able to get back to base and clean himself up while, true to form, Rob and Gav tucked into an al fresco pork fest at the Royal Standard, washed down with a couple of pints of Guinness.

The hot shower, paracetamol and coffee method seemed to work as a top-up to the partial recovery instigated by the fresh air and the all-too-brief kip on the beach, and so it was a passably sober Benedict who greeted his mum and dad in the Bell Cliff Tea Rooms.

They had spent all his childhood holidays in Lyme – he was an only child – and the tea rooms had been a reassuringly constant feature, with their nooks and crannies and uniformed waitresses.

When he and Sophie started to get serious, he brought her down to the 'Pearl of Dorset' to show her his old haunts and she fell for the place as comprehensively as he had as a young boy.

So, the wedding venue was a no-brainer, despite the initial protestations from Commander and Mrs Ward, who backed off from their insistence that the couple must get married in their parish church once Sophie had confirmed that she and Benedict would be footing the bill for the reception.

Like many of their generation, Cliff and Heather Mannion had been non-tactile parents, but they were trying as hard as they could to adapt to more modern practices.

They both offered awkward hugs before asking how their beloved son was feeling.

"Any last-minute nerves?" asked Cliff.

"We've just checked in to the Alexandra!" said Heather, with an air of girlish excitement.

The grand hotel had been way beyond their budget when Benedict was growing up. They normally stayed in a smaller establishment in Silver Street, or sometimes in a tiny holiday cottage just behind the seafront.

"I hope you took your mother's advice and had an early night," Cliff said.

"Of course," Ben replied. "I'm as ready as I can be!"

Inside, he was holding back tears. He hadn't told them either. His lovely, supportive mum and dad, who were so ridiculously proud of him.

***

The specialist had been empathetic but clear. When Benedict asked him the obvious question, he was told that he might have three years, five if he was lucky. There was no cure.

However, it was the advice that his condition would be largely invisible until much later on that was the catalyst for the massive deception that led him to his wedding day.

It had been all too easy to convince his darling Sophie that he was suffering from high blood pressure due to stress, and he even thanked her for making him seek medical advice. So, she never questioned his meds, and she trusted him, so she never read the packets.

He became skilled at hiding his appointments from her, taking spells of leave from work, and then hanging around art galleries until it was his normal time to finish up at the office.

As he habitually worked late, he would sometimes factor in a sneaky pint on the way back to avoid any comments from her about how good it was to see him getting home on time for a change.

Benedict had taught himself to become the arch deceiver. He had been due a regular medical for his firm's private insurers but had managed to arrange it for while he was on honeymoon. He couldn't stall them for ever, though.

But while he had just about managed to conceal the condition from his friends, as well as his work, he found it increasingly harder to complete a full round on the golf course – he could just about grit his teeth and get through it.

He'd have to invent some new plausible excuses, not easy when he loved the game so much.

"Well, we'd better get off, son. We thought we might have a walk down to the Cobb and then get ready for kick-off."

"Oh, Cliff," said Heather, "only you could compare your son's big day to a rugby match."

Benedict paid the bill and bid a temporary farewell to his folks.

How could he ever tell them? He would have to, but Sophie needed to know first. She must know first.

***

The rest of the day passed as a blur, as life's major events often do. Christenings, weddings, funerals, cup finals, all over before you know it.

Those so-called friends of his, Rob and Gav, had somehow managed to chalk 'HELP!' on the sole of one of his shoes, and 'DANGER! SOS!' on the other, which caused an outbreak of sniggering from the younger guests when the groom knelt before the celebrant.

The commander and Frantic Fran were horrified, while Cliff and Heather were too blissed-out to notice.

Sophie had never looked so stunning, and for a split second Benedict thought that he couldn't go through with it, he couldn't do this to the love of his life.

But he did go through with it because he lacked courage.

The reception was held in a marquee on the hotel lawn. The father of the bride gave a less-than-glowing reference to his son-in-law, starting out with an expression of regret that his elder daughter hadn't married one of a crop of promising naval officers that he and Frances had paraded in front of her.

Sophie, her face a picture of disgust and embarrassment, knew exactly why she was marrying Ben, his lack of a stiff military bearing being one among many reasons that she loved him.

"Anyway," boomed the commander, "I still have hopes for Emily!"

Realising from the complete lack of laughter or even appreciative murmuring that he had lost the room, the father of the bride made a token attempt to limit the damage by referring to Benedict's career prospects.

"Whilst I will never understand why my daughter chose an accountant over a naval officer, Ben has redeemed himself somewhat by having been offered a partnership. To my mind, a partnership is the pinnacle of professional achievement, so well done, son-in-law! But I still expect my tax affairs to be dealt with on a pro bono basis, ha ha!"

Ben glanced at Hugh and Verity, two of his new partners in the accountancy practice, who happened to be married to each other.

Their expressions gave nothing away, but he sensed that their first impressions of his father-in-law had matched his own. The man was just horrible.

Things were about to get worse, as the time had come for the best man's speech.

Remind me again, just why did I ask Rob? I must have been wasted, Benedict thought to himself as his oldest friend approached the microphone stand.

Rob Webber was good-looking and he knew it, his hair bleached by a childhood of surfing in Cornwall and more recent summers spent crewing in the Med, but his surface arrogance was tempered by a well-concealed but essentially kind nature, and Benedict was praying that he would be gentle with him today.

He needn't have worried. Rob was a barrister, and he knew how to respond to the summing up of opposing counsel.

"Ladies and gentlemen, the noble commander wishes that his daughter was marrying a naval officer. Well, in a manner of speaking, she is!"

Rob then clicked on his hand-held device, and a picture of Benedict appeared on the large screen behind him, in dress uniform. The stag weekend had *A Few Good Men*, the groom's favourite film, as its theme.

The guests oohed and aahed as Rob led them through a slide show of the groom's life to date, culminating in the formal engagement photo taken at the top of Primrose Hill.

"In conclusion, ladies, and gentlemen, what a legend of a man Benedict is. Kind, loyal, successful, and if anyone deserves to marry Sophie, he does."

The speech brought the house down, and as he struggled once more to hold back a river of tears, Ben knew exactly why he'd chosen Rob. And he even forgave him for leading him astray last night and for his part in defacing his shoes.

Then, suddenly, an unforgivable thought entered his head. *Perhaps Rob could be the person to comfort Sophie when the inevitable happened?*

He really, really must tell her on honeymoon. No more obfuscation. She'd understand, maybe not immediately, that he didn't want to spoil her big day.

***

Of course, he didn't tell her during the honeymoon. This was such a special time for the newlyweds, punctuating their urgent lovemaking with taking the bus down to Positano, or joining the hordes at Pompeii and Capri. The wine was pretty good too. The food was even better.

And he didn't tell her when they got back to their flat in Guildford, nor at their grisly first Christmas with the commander and Frantic Fran at their land-based gin palace in the harbourside village of Bosham, a somewhat-forced festive occasion which was chiefly memorable for a manly

Boxing Day chat with his father-in-law at the yacht club during which the commander learnt, to his horror, that his son-in-law didn't sail.

He would never understand what Sophie saw in Ben, but at least he was a partner in a Home Counties accountancy firm; he could have been a social worker or a town planner or a left-wing comprehensive schoolteacher. And he was a white heterosexual Englishman; thank God for small mercies.

Benedict didn't tell his parents either, but he did tell them the good news when Sophie was pregnant with Alfred. They were both thrilled, as, in a more downbeat fashion, were his in-laws.

The commander demanded to know if they knew the sex, and if it was a boy – "Then his name must be put down for the school!"

There were no complications with the birth. Alfred had a good pair of lungs on him and weighed in at a healthy nine pounds.

Having disappointed Fran and the commander by insisting on the Lyme Regis wedding, Ben and Sophie relented to the pressure and went along with the christening at Holy Trinity Church in Bosham.

Fran designed a christening gown that resembled an Edwardian sailor suit, and Rob and Emily made for lovely godparents. It was all lovely. Of course it was.

But Benedict was starting to feel weaker, both physically and morally.

It was, after all, at Bosham where Canute allegedly showed his nobles that even a king could not delay the inevitable; in his case, the turning of the tide, and as the photographer took an age to pose the happy family once they had emerged from the ancient church, the irony gradually dawned on the baby's father.

The Danish monarch had, of course, been correct – time and tide wait for no man, the inevitable will become reality.

But delay the real and the inevitable Benedict very deliberately did, for another summer, another Christmas and beyond Alfred's first birthday. He casually passed off the physical symptoms as exhaustion caused by becoming a new parent at the same time as having to prove his mettle as a freshly minted, in every way, partner in his firm.

He admitted to the paramedics that he was dying while he was still conscious in the ambulance, but he never told his wife or his parents, notwithstanding his dear mother being diagnosed with cancer just before Alfred's christening, and despite Sophie's anguished pleas for him to slow down at work, as she could see that he was going downhill.

Benedict may have succeeded in hiding his diagnosis from them until the end of his short life, but his wife and his young child would face a desperate future trying to live with the consequences of his toxic cowardice.

Awaiting

The confirmation of the pregnancy was the news they had been waiting for, but the timing wasn't the best.

Edmund's latest exhibition had been cancelled during the pandemic, and with it the lingering hope of a shot at national recognition.

Of course, it was different for artists – they could be discovered later in their careers, or even posthumously, but this offered scant comfort. Edmund and Sarah had bills to cover in the grim world of the present.

There was an outside chance that the exhibition might be rescheduled, now that lockdown was becoming a receding memory, but they would have to come up with something concrete; a plan, before the baby was born, or else penury beckoned.

***

The couple had met at art college in Plymouth.

Edmund had grown up in Dawlish, on the South Devon coast, where his parents ran an old-fashioned ladies and gentlemen's outfitters.

He was a solitary child, taking himself off for walks around the town, collecting interesting bits of driftwood from the beaches.

He would leave them to dry out, then varnish them and sell them to tourists, his first profitable artistic venture.

The early closing sign was put out on Wednesdays, these being the last few years when shops could close early, before the liberalisation of shopping hours, Sunday opening, and a plethora of innovations that Edmund's parents, Methodists both, abhorred.

Edmund's father, Cyril Weaver, used to go up to Exeter on Wednesday afternoons, sometimes to see his accountant or maybe for a check-up at the dentists, but more often than not to look at material in the warehouses.

At half terms and school holidays, he'd bring young Ed along for the ride and, as the wholesale warehouses were around the corner from Exeter Art Gallery and Museum, he would leave his son there to mooch around.

A whole world of possibility seemed to open up to the nascent young artist as he ambled around the galleries, open-mouthed in innocent amazement and sheer joy.

He was impressed by a vast painting called *Curtius Leaping into the Gulf* by Benjamin Haydon, but it was the excellent collection of English watercolours that really fired his imagination and led him to his vocation.

Artists like Samuel Prout, William Payne of Plymouth, Widgery and Francis Towne.

This early fascination paid dividends, as, by the time that he had left art college, Ed felt that he was starting to find his artistic feet, anchored in the safe harbour and warm embrace of his native southwest.

Sarah, by contrast, was from Winchester where her father worked as a legal executive in the property department of Hampshire County Council, based in the large building known as The Castle, which appears to stare down rather grumpily over the city from the Upper High Street.

Her mother was a nurse at the Winchester Royal, just up from the Castle on the Romsey Road.

Both of Sarah's parents had come of age in the sixties, and they had clung on to the positive vibes of their formative years.

Sarah was one of three children, tall and blonde, the youngest, and she enjoyed an idyllic childhood exploring the water meadows and riverside walks, encouraged in her wanderings by her arty parents.

It was from these explorations that she began to sketch wildlife, and by her teens she had graduated to pen and ink drawings of the cathedral, the butter cross and her favourite part of town, towards the bottom of St Swithun Street, where the rarefied worlds of the cathedral and the college seem to merge into one.

Sarah was well taught by her art teachers at the King's School, and later at Peter Symonds, and was encouraged to apply to the top London academies.

But she was single-minded. She wanted to study somewhere where inspiration was out there on the doorstep, and where she could be close to the ocean.

Her parents had told her about Dartington Hall, near Totnes, where they had used up their annual leave by attending summer school before the children were born.

The Hall's future was in some doubt when it came to choosing where to read for her degree, but Plymouth looked interesting. It was a large city, bang on the border between Devon and Cornwall, so she would discover plenty to see, and to draw, within easy reach.

The idea of being in a larger place than Winchester, that snuggly comfort blanket of a city for the liberal middle classes, sounded appealing and Plymouth didn't sound like a scary place to perch for three or four years, unlike London or one of the northern cities.

So, Plymouth Art College it was, and it turned out just fine, even though there were some quite lairy areas to avoid.

She made friendships that would last for years to come, and, in her second year she noticed a certain Edmund Weaver, who was on the master's course.

He was good-looking, but charmingly unaware of it, and when she admitted to her flatmates Jess and Hannah that she was interested in him, they both laughed and told her that Ed had many admirers, but that he never let anyone close to him.

Sarah took this as a challenge.

Edmund, for his part, was instantly attracted to Sarah and was surprised and flattered to be approached by her in the college canteen, and even more taken aback when he seemed to be abducted by an alien force that took over his power of speech.

Later that evening, he couldn't quite believe that he had told her about his forthcoming exhibition, let alone asked her to come to the modest opening.

With a delicious coincidence, the exhibition was to be held in the very same Exeter gallery where he used to spend his happiest moments, those wonderful Wednesday afternoons when his father was visiting the warehouses.

He knew that he had only been booked to fill a short gap in the calendar, but it was still the pinnacle of his career so far.

Titled 'Edmund Weaver: a West Country Journey', the exhibition featured a selection of his watercolours, mainly of Dartmoor and the South Hams, with the occasional foray into North Devon and Cornwall.

As he and Sarah headed to the gallery on the train to Exeter St Davids, another significant character was waiting on the London-bound platform after a meeting with the Bishop of Exeter.

The Reverend Roy Swettenham had grown up in Bideford, North Devon and came from a similar small-business background to that of Edmund.

In his late forties and seemingly fated to remain single, he had been a popular and successful parish priest in the Midlands, and latterly in a gently prosperous corner of Berkshire.

But he was aching to return to his roots in the west.

He'd been in contact with the Bishop of Exeter for a while – he had been taught by him at theological college – and now his old friend and tutor had summoned him for a meeting, as he had said, "I may have something for you."

That something was the parish of Totnes, the administrative centre of the beautiful South Hams area, close to Dartington Hall.

The bishop confided in Reverend Roy that he had immediately thought of him when the benefice became vacant. Roy was a keen and accomplished amateur artist and he would fit in well with the arty, bordering on hipster, vibe of the place.

Feeling encouraged and even excited as he left the afternoon meeting, Roy decided to have a look at the art gallery before heading back to the station.

And that is how he came to view the works of a promising Devon artist, and how he would, in time, become his unlikely patron and benefactor.

***

It was the one picture that did it – *Hidden Depths*.

This was an abstract representation of a dark, seemingly disused boat, with sand dunes forming the backdrop.

The tide was in, and a shoal of fish was just visible underneath the hull. A mysterious hut or small house appeared in the top left-hand corner of the composition.

Roy was mesmerised and knew that he had to have it. Time would prove him right, as he spent decades enjoying the picture, constantly discovering new aspects and interpretations.

The museum accepted his post-dated cheque for the deposit – the cashless society had yet to take hold – and so it was a delighted Edmund who saw that a red 'sold' sticker had already appeared on one his works when he arrived for the reception.

The gallery ran to some posh crisps and warm white wine, and it was hardly rammed for the opening, but there were some murmurs of interest, and he was interviewed on Radio Devon.

And he'd sold a painting, one of the pricier of those on display.

The coming years saw Roy being offered the Totnes

job, where he settled in remarkably quickly and grew the congregation by simply being a good parish priest who people warmed to.

Edmund and Sarah married in Winchester Register Office, and they started their new life in her parents' converted attic.

Sarah soon found a job teaching at Winchester Art College, which paid for some studio space in a converted barn development just outside Stockbridge.

Ed exhibited in the Wykeham Gallery in Stockbridge High Street, and he was gaining in reputation after successful shows in Alresford and Petersfield, but it was an uncertain life. If he sold just one painting at a prestige gallery it felt like a lottery win, but the winnings had to be eked out, and, if possible, ploughed back into the business.

He and Sarah put on a joint show of their work in Devizes, where her pen and ink comparisons of Salisbury and Winchester cathedrals became a brief sensation.

However, Ed was missing the inspirational landscape of the southwest – he found it hard to be moved by the Test and Itchen Valleys as he found them too twee, too chocolate box to get excited about.

Sarah's parents were lovely, and genuinely enjoyed having them around, but the younger couple needed a place of their own and they wouldn't be able to afford much in the golden triangle around Winchester.

They began to hatch a plan to move back to Devon. Much of the county had become scarily expensive – although nowhere near as much as Hampshire – but they could afford to buy in Plymouth, at least to get their feet on the ladder.

They still knew a few people down there from art

school days, and they had heard about ambitious plans for a spanking new arts complex called The Box, where they could both apply for work.

And as they already knew, the city was a base from which they could scour the surrounding region for inspiration.

Then it happened. First, the initial story about a virus in some random place in China, then Italian ski resorts being closed and finally the UK eventually waking up to the danger after the pox-infested Cheltenham Festival of March 2020.

Sarah was furloughed from the college. Painting was not an essential occupation, so Ed had to lock up the space in Stockbridge and his long-anticipated exhibition at the Pallant Gallery in Chichester was cancelled.

Sarah's dad cleared his shed, which they made into a makeshift studio, but the pandemic period was a period of anxiety and waiting, waiting, waiting.

Like several other artists, Ed's style morphed during this period. His work had become lighter, more hopeful somehow after he met his soulmate, but it veered off into dark places as the shutdown seemed to be in danger of becoming permanent.

At least Reverend Roy continued to buy his work, always paying a deposit and then the balance in monthly instalments. He had become the largest private collector of Ed's pictures, for which Ed and Sarah, atheists both, thanked the Lord or whoever or whatever had drawn the lovely priest to the Exeter show all those years ago.

Then, just as the country stumbled out of the lockdowns, blinking uncertainly into the light of day, Sarah discovered that she was expecting. A lockdown baby, a little miracle.

They had wanted a family but hadn't planned for this new

arrival. Perhaps the ennui of the blank world from which they had just emerged had led to them forgetting to take precautions? Or maybe the precautions just hadn't worked – nothing was foolproof in this life.

As they started to discuss what to do about having a baby, it struck them both that they were, in effect, drawing up a pro and con list, which seemed somewhat callous when the subject was the survival or otherwise of a potential life.

Nevertheless, it did help them to decide to keep the child. The arguments against, which included the ethics of bringing a baby into a world of war, pandemic, global warming and horrid nationalist governments, lost out to the overwhelming feeling that this was somehow right and meant to be. They would be good parents, as both of theirs had been.

And despite the inevitable worry and financial impact, they eventually admitted to each other that they were thrilled with the news.

Of course, once they had accepted this and told their parents, the realities crowded in, the urgent one being lack of money.

Sarah was the steady breadwinner, with Ed chipping in the odd bonus when he managed to sell a painting.

While her parents would be happy to look after the little one while Sarah was out at work, this wasn't, if they were honest, what any of them wanted. Certainly not in the long-term.

***

One dull day in early summer, Ed was back working in the studio near Stockbridge when he took a call from Rev. Roy.

"Ed, you old scoundrel," the vicar of Totnes yelled down the line, "I know you want to keep it to yourself, but I must have it!"

'It' was *Evening Light*, an early Edmund Weaver monotype that Roy had coveted since that first exhibition in Exeter, and he had been reminded of it at Ed's last show before lockdown.

The artist was tempted, as he could use the money, but the picture was dear to him, as it was based on a visit to North Devon with Sarah when they were both students. They were the shadowy couple shown embracing under the lychgate.

He told his most loyal supporter that he would talk it over with Sarah, but no promises.

Roy, the quintessential pastor, turned the conversation to the couple's well-being and Ed told him about the new arrival. He knew that Sarah wouldn't mind, as Roy was almost family, so central had he become to their livelihood, and he soon found himself unburdening his worries for the future on his wise counsellor.

The conversation haunted the kindly parson, and it was on one of his early morning walks through Totnes that he came up with the makings of a plan.

Having given himself a few days to mull and finesse, he called Ed again.

"Sorry to press you, old chap, but any thoughts about *Evening Light*?"

Ed began to dissemble, at which point Roy burst out laughing.

"Look, I do have an idea, which does concern the picture in a way. I thought I might pay a visit to Winchester soon. I have an aged aunt in a nursing home just outside the city at Headbourne Worthy and I've just heard that she is starting to fade, so I thought I'd call in on you on my way back, if we can agree a date? Splendid! I can stay over at my cousin's in Andover."

***

Roy's plan worked. The delayed new arts complex in Plymouth was due to open in the following year, and they wanted an artist-in-residence.

Roy was plugged into the Devon and Cornwall arts scene, and so he immediately thought of his protégé.

The conversation with Ed led to the meeting in Winchester and Roy unveiled his plan with a flourish.

He would be delighted to put Ed's name forward for the new role at The Box. After all, his young friend had an inbuilt advantage as an alumnus of the art college as well as his growing, albeit stalled, reputation.

Whether Edmund was successful in his application or not, Roy offered both of them the use of a substantial part of his vicarage, in which he currently rattled around like a pea in a drum.

He wouldn't require rent, but he did want something – *Evening Light*. Roy persuaded Ed that he only wanted the picture on loan. He had a place reserved for it on his study wall, so he could see it while he wrote his sermons, and Ed, of course, would be able to view it whenever he wanted to.

So, ten weeks later, with the baby still three months away, we find Ed and Sarah safely ensconced in Totnes with Roy.

They have their own self-contained space; Ed starts work as artist-in-residence at The Box in the new year and inspiration gradually returns to him as he settles back like a sunbathing seal in his beloved Devon.

Roy is enjoying the couple's convivial company and is loving sharing his study with *Evening Light*, however temporarily.

As for Sarah, she is looking forward to the birth with renewed confidence, delighted that their child will be a Devonshire dumpling.

Looking out from their top-floor window as the soothing balm of the gentle breeze melds with the last glimpse of the evening light as it commences its dreamy descent over the Dart Valley, she thinks back to those days of pandemic despair, when life seemed to be about waiting, waiting, waiting.

This was very different. It was the hope of life itself. Awaiting, awaiting, awaiting.

The Price of Love

They were spoilt for choice; there were so many places where they could break the familiar long journey. There was the posh farm shop with the lovely café, there was the time-warp '70s-style short-order greasy spoon near the petrol station just off the A30.

Then again, they could save money by using their National Trust memberships and stop at Killerton or Castle Drogo (*Castle Drongo* as the kids used to call it), or they could try Roadford Lake.

They hadn't been there for a good few years and Rex had heard that that the facilities were much better now. There were new loos, the food offering had been scaled up and you could sit outside and take in the view of the lake, if the weather was up to it.

"What do you think, love? It's glorious, and we should have missed the lunch crowd by now. I reckon we could treat ourselves to an al fresco cream tea. Get us in the mood."

He turned to the passenger seat.

"Great, we are at one! I'll get us there in no time!"

Roadford Lake is a reservoir that doubles as a tourist attraction, with enviable views of the Devon countryside.

After struggling with the parking app, he found a table on the terrace and ordered two cream teas. "It's a bit breezy out on the lake – look at those windsurfers go! Don't you wish we were young again!"

A young waiter, probably from the local sixth-form college, brought out their cream tea for two.

"Enjoy!" he said, as he had no doubt been trained to do.

"I always feel like replying 'I might do, I haven't tasted it yet'," said Rex.

"Now be careful, love, we are in Devon; so cream first, jam on top."

***

After a slow second part of the journey, caused by roadworks near Truro, they finally arrived at their regular bolthole, the little hotel on a bend of the Helford River.

As Rex opened the boot and heaved out their suitcases, he looked around.

"Where are they? The Lurch twins?"

The aforementioned twins were, in fact, the hotel's long-serving and, it had to be admitted, lugubrious general factotums. They were not related to each other, but one of Rex and Gillian's naughty children – it was probably Timothy – had christened them the Lurch twins, and Rex always had to bite his tongue so as not to giggle when one of them lurched into view.

The appearance of one or other Lurch would also be a cue for the kids to click their fingers in tribute to the Addams family theme, or put on a deep voice and say, "You rang?" before scarpering off, sniggering, to a safe hiding place.

On one notorious occasion, Christine, the youngest and best behaved of the three siblings, approached the elder of the two porters and said, "Oi, Lurch, is the tennis court free this morning?"

Her brothers, Timothy and Jeremy, were, of course, blamed for egging her on and putting ideas in her head.

A confident young man suddenly appeared at Rex's side, as if he been teleported there.

"Welcome to Cornwall, sir. Can I take your luggage?"

"Come on, love," said Rex.

After reassuring him that the luggage would be taken straight to the room, the lady at reception, who didn't sound remotely Cornish, asked to see Rex's credit card, and then confirmed the dinner reservation for two people at 7:30pm.

She showed him up to the bedroom, which had been given the twenty-first-century treatment since they had last been there. He was dismayed to be given a swipe card instead of a proper key, but the room was lovely, and they had a view of the path leading to the river. There was even a little balcony where they could sit with their tea and admire the scenery.

Rex struggled to open the glass balcony door, but once he had succeeded, he turned around and said, "Just breathe in that air! This is what we have missed during all that Covid nonsense. We won't have any trouble sleeping tonight."

After a quick cuppa, and then snoozing off the journey, it was suddenly time for dinner.

"You look a picture, my angel," said Rex.

The dinner table offered a decent view of the river and as Rex took off his glasses to give them a good polish prior to getting down to the serious business of reading the menu and wine list, a shy little tear ran down his cheek.

"Are you alright, sir?" said the sommelier, another staff member who was clearly in on the teleporting thing.

"Oh! Yes, miles away. We have been coming to this hotel every year since we got married, so I always get sentimental. Gillian thinks I'm a big softy."

"I expect you have seen some changes then, sir?"

Rex considered enquiring after the Lurches, but instead told the sommelier that they both liked the recent changes, especially the modern shower in their room.

"I will let the owners know, sir. Now, have you had time to look at the wine list?"

Rex most certainly had, and ordered two glasses of the petit Chablis, which the sommelier told him was an excellent choice.

Rex and Gillian were both having the hake, freshly landed at Newlyn that very morning.

Another waiter brought the wine and asked Rex if he wanted to taste it.

"My wife is the expert, but she's just gone to the powder room, so yes, I am sure I can be trusted!"

"Brave of you, sir," said the waiter as he went through the ritual pantomime.

Rex supressed a giggle as he remembered when the Lurch twins used to wait on tables.

'Wine? Red or white?' had been the limit of their sales patter, delivered in a somewhat threatening manner.

The food appeared a little late, but Rex excused this as they were probably understaffed in the kitchen, as everywhere seemed to be after the pandemic.

His children blamed Brexit for these sorts of problems, but he wasn't so sure. He had never dared admit to them that he had voted leave, and he hadn't even told Gillian, who he suspected wanted to remain.

Rex took his time over the food, seemingly in something of a trance, which he snapped out of when he became aware of a couple at the adjoining table.

"Just ignore their funny looks, Gill. They probably feel outclassed. Fancy not wearing a tie to dinner. And you are quite right, love. She's wearing jeans. Probably got a tattoo or two. That was rather witty wasn't it – a tattoo or two!"

The young waiter was hovering, and asked Rex if he could clear the plates.

"I'm sorry that your wife didn't eat her meal. Was there an issue? Can I get her something else, perhaps?"

Rex explained that Gillan had been feeling a bit peaky, so she had gone back to the room. He declined a dessert but had a coffee before signing for the bill.

The bedroom was up a steep staircase, so Rex was out of breath when he got there and was muttering about the uselessness of the swipe card key when one of the staff came by and showed him how it worked.

Once safely in, he undressed in the en suite, cleaned his teeth and snuggled into bed.

"Happy anniversary, love. Sleep tight. If the weather holds, perhaps we can go to Trebah Gardens after breakfast? Be lovely to see it again."

A Few Weeks Earlier

The modest little village church was packed for the funeral

and the traffic in the high street was momentarily halted as the hearse led the mourners to the burial ground, situated up the lane from the church itself.

Rex had gone ahead and was already waiting at the graveside with the vicar and the undertaker's assistants, and so the children led the procession.

Falling into step with Jeremy, Christine gingerly asked him how their father was coping as he was the only one who had remained in the area after university and he and his wife Brid had been tireless in their support of Rex as Gillian was fading.

"That's just it. I don't think he is coping. He's acting as if she is still alive."

"That's what I was worried about. They loved each other so much, and loved us so much, that he must be in denial. He's paying a huge price."

"What do you mean?"

"Haven't you heard the expression 'grief is the price you pay for love'? Well, Dad loved Mum so much that the price in his case is incalculable."

Timothy, who had been comforting his children, caught the end of the conversation. "It's going to be beyond tough for him. What can we do?"

"Be there for him. Be kind and start repaying all the love he gave us."

"But how long is this going to go on for? He has just told me that they are going back to their old haunt in Cornwall for their anniversary…"

The Autumn Men

I'd love to be an Autumn Man
apple cheeks and woodsmoke hair
voluntary work all done
the well-earned pint and lunchtime pie
and noticing when trudging home
the last of this year's geese have flown
the *pale autumnal sky*

From *Autumn Men* by Adrian Crick

The rowdy lads of spring became the boys of summer, but they were overripe, russet-tinted autumn men now: Clarky, Browner, Toby and Jonno.

Well into autumn as it goes, as they were meeting up for a belated celebration of Clarky's sixtieth.

The friendship had started at university and had developed over the intervening years, up and down the snakes and ladders of careers and family life – mostly downs in the case of Clarky in recent times – in good health and bad and despite all the awful world events that had been going on in the background.

Browner, who was also known to the group as Captain Sensible, arrived a day later than the other three. Clarky and Toby had got there late on Thursday night, driving down from London after work, and Jonno had joined them on the Friday, one of his 'shirking from home' days.

Captain Sensible left the house before 6am on the Saturday morning, taking great care not to disturb Chloe and their youngest, Harry, who was still at home.

He had several reasons for arriving last, the practical one being that he was a teacher, a deputy head at a huge Portsmouth comprehensive, so he couldn't simply take days off in term time.

But his main reason for keeping things as short as possible was that he couldn't handle the excessive drinking anymore so, by avoiding the first couple of nights, he hoped he could miss the worst of it.

Fond as he was of his old mates, if he was honest, he'd been gradually growing away from them.

The others had given him untold grief at their last reunion when he had the temerity to suggest that perhaps the time had come to invite other halves, maybe stay in a spa hotel in Cornwall he'd read about in *The Guardian*, which led to his sad realisation that the other guys still really loved, well, just being guys.

They looked forward to these weekends like kids looked forward to Christmas, whereas he hated being away from Chloe.

The old Elton John song 'I Guess That's Why They Call It the Blues' always came to mind when he was missing her.

He was a reflective man, Browner.

Clarky wasn't, as a rule. He was the character of the group, the one that people remembered.

At his cash-building City pomp, he would enter any social gathering and robustly advise anyone foolish enough to be within earshot that he was there to shag all the women and fight all the men. He never came close to succeeding in this mission as he was habitually either too drunk or coked-up to put such plans into practise, but also because, at base, it was mere bravado.

He may have been the noisy one, but he was the only one who had never settled down, not that this seemed to bother him. Nothing really bothered him. He'd got out of high-octane banking in his forties and these days he was happy to just sit back and enjoy the remnants of his massive fortune.

Jonno was the group's resident jock, a rugger blue, a competitive golfer and still a regular marathon runner as he approached the big six-zero.

The others were never very clear about exactly what Jonno did; he described himself as a consultant, but however he made a living, it had paid the school fees for the kids, funded amazing homes in London and the Algarve and a new car every year since he was twenty-five. He was the petrolhead of the gang.

"What are you consulting this time, your arsehole?" was repeated by Clarky with tedious annual regularity.

Then there was Toby. He was the Sherpa, the one who kept the team going, who organised the weekends, who had set up the WhatsApp group.

He was also the main reason that Browner still attended after all these years, as Tobes had been his closest friend at university, best man at his wedding, and, unlike the other two, he had reined in the serious drinking.

Toby was in the middle of the group financially – he had never made serious money like Jonno or Clarky but had made a decent living in publishing and his long-term partner was a reasonably well-known ITN reporter.

He could always be relied upon to defend poor Browner when he was being roasted by the other two for going into teaching, for being an Arsenal-supporting *Guardian* reader, for voting to remain, preferring football to rugby or for calling it a night before the serious post-pub whisky drinking got underway.

So, as he turned into the driveway of the sumptuous holiday let that Tobes had arranged – or 'taken for the weekend' as he put it – Browner was determined that this would be the very last time.

That determination was reinforced somewhat by the delightful sounds of retching that greeted him as he stepped out of his modest Toyota.

A grinning Clarky was there to greet him on the doorstep. He said, "You missed a mega sesh last night! I'm afraid Toby couldn't hack the pace! Just listen to him honking up! Brilliant! Hey, remember *The Fast Show*? 'Isn't honking up *brilliant!*' Come on, I'll give you the tour. It's bloody huge, so we've all got suites."

Browner's sense of trepidation deepened; the best thing about these get togethers was the walking, but although he was more than ready for a hike after a long week and an early morning drive down, only stopping at a lay-by for a coffee and a bacon roll, his bedraggled fellow campers looked as if they had only just got themselves up.

Jonno was sitting in the kitchen mainlining champagne from the bottle – 'hair of the dog, old man' – and Toby was clearly the worse for wear, which left Clarky.

"So, when are we setting off along the coast path?" Browner asked him, more in hope than expectation.

It was a glorious crisp early November morning, the sea would be glistening in the sunlight, there would still be a frost on the ground and if they managed their normal walk they would get to the Dolphin in time for lunch and a well-earned pie and a pint.

"Hmm," said Clarky, "thing is, we thought we'd drive this time. Walking is all very well, good for the mental elf and all that nonsense, but if we drive, we can get to more pubs. Jonno has brought his new baby down with him – it's in the garage – and he's devised this route called the Devon Seven. It's going to be epic! Get in!"

"You are not seriously suggesting that Jonno is in a fit state to drive? And seven pubs! Why don't I drive you all – I don't mind missing the beers."

"What! You've come all this way to sip mineral water? No way, Browner, you sad little man, it's all for one!"

"Well, let's get a taxi then. We can easily afford to hire one for the day."

"Typical socialist idea! You'll be suggesting that we use public transport next. Anyway, have you ever seen a taxi down here? And you don't have to worry about the cops – once we are away from the main road, Jonno will be barrelling down the lanes at twice the speed of sound, and we can go way off-road in that thing, so it isn't a problem."

"But what if Jonno barrels into something coming the other way?"

"Simples. They come off worse."

"Know what? You can count me out. I'm walking the coast path on my own."

As Browner was pointedly filling his water bottle in the utility room, he was joined by Toby, who seemed to have made a remarkable recovery.

"I'll come with you," he said. "The last thing I need is more time with those two, and have you seen that glorious weather?"

The first part of the walk was quite steep, but as they reached the clifftop, they had a good flat stretch ahead of them and the old friends soon fell into easy conversation.

"So, what happened last night? And how come you seem OK now? You were vomiting for England when I arrived."

"I exaggerated it a bit, as I wanted an excuse to get out of Jonno's mad Seven of Devon or whatever he called it. But I had been ill."

"I hope Jonno left his 'baby' at home when you ventured out last night?"

Toby stopped to retie his walking boots at the next stile, so they both took the chance for a breather and to look out to sea.

"We went to the Pilchard. We walked over the causeway, but then the tide came in when we were three pints down – my absolute limit is two these days – and so we had to get them to call the sea tractor."

"So why were you so ill?"

"Too much salt."

"They didn't chuck you overboard?"

Toby laughed. "No, but I wouldn't have put it past those two idiots. One of them, probably Clarky, tipped the entire contents of a salt cellar into my pint while I was having a pee."

"That old college trick. Hilarious."

"I drank gallons of water before I turned in, but still felt as if I'd been swimming the channel when I got up, so I forced myself to be sick to get rid of the sludge that was left in my stomach. Another pint of cold water and I was starting to feel human again, and this Devon air is working wonders."

"I take it that the lords of misrule didn't limit themselves to three pints?"

"Oh no, they got stuck into the single malt."

"Oh well, their loss. What a view!"

Back at the five-star accommodation, Jonno was checking his Patek Phillipe.

"Opening time at Ringmore in twenty minutes! Come on, Clarky, get your arse in gear!"

***

The walk to the Dolphin was punctuated by an agreeable blend of conversation and companionable silences.

It turned out that Tobes had also been harbouring doubts about coming down, despite having organised the long weekend, admittedly under pressure from Jonno and Clarky.

He said, "Unlike them, I do possess the necessary skill set to organise a piss-up in a brewery. But seriously, I took some persuading this year."

"Who by?" said Browner.

"Sash. She's covering *News at Ten* this weekend, so I wouldn't be seeing much of her, and she said I shouldn't leave you to cope with those two without backup."

"Well, tell her that she was right. Seriously, mate, I think this is the last time. Get me out of here."

"Me too. Remember when you suggested other halves? I thought it was a good idea. Haven't we grown out of the male-bonding thing?"

Browner looked reflective. He said, "I never grew into it, if I'm being truthful. But yeah, I was taken aback by the angry reaction. I suppose Clarky might have felt left out, although I expect he'd have found some impressionable young thing to bring down with him."

"But Jonno?" Tobes replied. "I do wonder about him and Angelique – they never seem to do anything together."

"Sasha and Chloe always get on well…"

"So why don't we four do it next time?" said Tobes.

"Agreed. But who is going to break it to Jonno and Clarky?"

The two friends fell silent as they reached another incline, then they stopped for a drink of water when they reached the wide estuary of the River Erme.

Browner broke the silence. "This is going to sound a bit deep but what do you think has kept us going for all these years? And why did we hit it off so well all that time ago?"

Toby gave one of his lop-sided grins. "Very philosophical, Captain Sensible. But you are right. What did draw us together? It's not as if we all have much in common these days. I mean, we do, but Clarky and Jonno…"

"Have we drifted apart, or was there anything there in the first place?"

***

Jonno screeched up to the little pub on the stroke of opening time and parked directly outside, with no lack of ostentation or entitlement.

He and Clarky were the first customers of the day.

"Two pints of your best foaming ale, squire! Ha ha!" Clarky shouted at the perplexed Ukrainian bartender.

They downed a further two each before speeding off to the next unsuspecting hostelry.

A middle-aged couple, who had been trying to enjoy a quiet lunch, asked to see the landlord.

"Did you see that, George? Those two posh morons have just driven off. They were both putting it away, so I think you should call the police."

***

As they recommenced their walk, turning inland towards the village of Kingston, Tobes and Browner continued with their philosophical debate.

"I think I may have the answer – we hit it off because we all hated the same people. The politicos in the Union, the hearty private-dining club Bullingdon wannabees, the swots who spent all their time in the library. The neanderthal rowers."

"You are right – was there anyone we didn't despise?"

"But now, seriously, what do we really have in common?"

They walked on purposefully, both seemingly deep in thought, until the roof of the sixteenth-century inn hove into view.

"Tobes, you don't think Jonno and Clarky have actually set out on their stupid pub tour, do you?"

"Christ! I'd been enjoying the walk and our chat so much that I'd forgotten all about the Devon Seven. Look, we know we can get reception in the pub, I'll call Jonno and make sure they stay put."

Having tugged off their muddy boots and squeezed into a cosy nook near the fire, Toby went to the bar, returning with two pints of Jail Ale.

Browner had been on the phone. "I've tried both of them – straight to voicemail."

"I can't believe that they could be so irresponsible, but what can we do? By the time we get back it will be late afternoon and we don't know which pubs they are visiting."

"I think we should have a quick sandwich here and head straight back before it gets dark. If they are out, we can drive to the places we do know, see if they've been there."

"Yeah, the locals would remember Clarky if he pitched up. Once met, never forgotten."

"Or we could always ask them here."

"What, if they remember two pissed-up idiots disrupting their peace and quiet?"

"Why not? At least we should warn them that Jonno and Clarky are careering around the lanes."

"Or we could call the police. There is a limit to friendship. What if they caused an accident?"

"Which we could have prevented? OK, I'll talk to the landlord. But the police? I'm not sure I could do that."

The landlord, who was announced over the inn's magnificent oak door as David Ayres, licensed to serve beers wines and spirits, put in a call to Pub Watch, a service that warned nearby establishments of possible trouble in the area.

Ayres said that they hardly ever needed it down here, not like in Torquay and Plymouth.

He called Totnes Police Station as well, thus sparing Toby and Browner from having to make the difficult decision whether to report their friends to the authorities.

Ayres could sense that the two of them were shaken up, and so suggested that they finished off their lunch and then headed back. "You've done all you can do, chaps. Chances are that your friends have left the car at home anyway. Be a shame to bugger up your walk for nothing. It's the best day we've had since the summer."

***

The return walk was conducted in an atmosphere of brooding silence, in direct contrast to the companionable version they had shared on the outward journey along that breathtaking slice of the southwest coastal footpath.

The weather was beginning to reflect the mood of the walkers, as darkening skies led to a soaking rain as they reached Challaborough.

Captain Sensible was the first to notice the police car parked opposite the swish house in Bigbury-on-Sea.

"It looks like the friendly landlord was wrong. Why would the police be outside if Jonno had left the SUV in the garage?"

"We don't know that, Browner. Come on, we will be there in five minutes."

As the weary friends trudged up the hill, they were approached by two uniformed officers.

"Good evening, gentlemen. Are you staying at this house?"

"Er, yes," said a hesitant Toby. "We've taken it for the weekend."

"Very good. In that case, can we come inside?"

The policeman made the formal introductions. "I am PC Steven Tilley, and this is my colleague PC Karen Smale. And you are?"

"Sorry, Officer, I should have said. Tobias Hunter, and this is my friend Simon Browne."

"And are you staying here together or are there more of you?" asked Karen Smale.

"There are. Peter Clarke and Jonathan Darnley," Browner replied.

"In that case, sir," said PC Tilley, "I have some serious news for you."

"You may want to sit down."

***

Jonno and Clarky had managed to complete four legs of the Devon Seven, despite having been reported by several landlords as well as by their friends.

A couple of walkers sitting outside the Cricketers in Beesands had taken a picture of Jonno's personalised number plate and the landlord had tipped off the police, having already been put on his guard by David Ayres at the Dolphin.

Overhearing whispered conversations at the bar and correctly sensing that their number was up, Jonno ran into the car park followed by Clarky, who he hauled into the passenger seat as the vehicle was moving.

Jonno's playlist had reached 'Song 2' by Blur, which

blasted from the open windows as they made their escape.

The driver, noticing a gap in the hedge, ploughed into the field at speed and then crashed through a partially locked but rickety farm gate at the far side, the bull bar limiting the damage to the vehicle.

"Woo hah!" they both yelled along to the music.

"We're fine now," said Jonno as they reached a greenway. "We can just bimble down these lanes, and then we can turn into the main road for the last few yards."

"Jesus!" said Clarky. "Where did they come from?"

A police car had been strategically parked up in a passing place to await the SUV and was now following them.

"All guns blazing, Clarky!" yelled Jonno as he put his foot down.

***

Back at the house, PC Smale explained that the chase had ended when the car ploughed into a farm vehicle, injuring the driver. The occupants of the SUV suffered serious injuries and needed to be cut out with specialist equipment and then airlifted to Derriford Hospital.

"I am afraid that Mr Clarke did not survive the collision, Mr Darnley is still alive, but in a critical condition."

Epilogue

Jonno was saved by his superior fitness but spent the rest of his life in a wheelchair, requiring constant medical attention. His wife, the icy Angelique, who had never in her life turned right when boarding a plane, bailed out after six months. He was sentenced to a jail term but was pronounced medically unfit to serve it.

He blamed Browner and Toby for dobbing him in. They never spoke again and Angelique, with a breathtaking lack of concern for his future medical needs, and the huge costs involved, instructed her lawyers to take him to the cleaners.

Captain Sensible and Tobes remain the best of friends, all too happy to morph into frosted winter men, and they and their partners spend regular, cheerful times away together, but never in Devon.

The Comeback

"That was Chris Rea with 'Road to Hell', played specially for Derek and Sandra from Peverell. Hope that brought back some memories, guys. Now, my star guest is a real, living legend, the one and only Shane Meredith! Come on, we all remember the '70s, don't we? When Shane got to the top of the charts with 'Stuck on the Subs' Bench of Love'?"

His producer shrugged, as he clearly had no recollection of Mr Meredith or his celebrated back catalogue.

"So don't go anywhere, we'll be right back with Shane after these messages!"

***

Shane Meredith was born in 1959 and was christened Nicholas Raymond Willis.

He came into the world too late for Elvis and Buddy Holly, but he was just in time for Sgt Pepper's, so he worshipped The Beatles. He formed his first group (never bands in those far-off days), with two mates from Public Secondary, Tony Finch (drums) and Kev Lyons (bass).

For reasons that are lost in the annals of rock history,

they went by the groovy name of 'Nicky and the Nightshift'.

By the time he had left school to work in the gents' clothes department at Dingles, he had formed and disbanded several groups, and at the age of twenty he made the hard decision to go solo, as the age of the sensitive singer songwriter had arrived.

He was going to be the James Taylor of the southwest.

However, this meant terminating his exclusive songwriting partnership with Steve Bomyer, so he issued a press release which announced to a shocked world that Devon's version of Lennon and McCartney was no more.

Steve, devastated, joined the navy and the pair never met again.

***

"Welcome back, crew! Now, I hope you are sitting comfortably as I am super stoked to welcome… Shane Meredith!"

"It's great to be here, Craig. You know, it feels spookily like home."

"Well, I guess it is – you started out round the corner from this very studio if my researchers have got it right!"

"Yeah, it was a different world then, such a great time."

"OK, so take me back. You always wanted to play music?"

"Yeah, and write songs, you know. The best thing about school was leaving it."

"But a little bird told me that it was your primary school teacher who gave you the idea for your name?"

"Yeah. Miss Meredith. She was a real chick."

"Er, OK, Shane. Let's go back to your glory days. Tell

me about when you reached the top of the Plymouth Hit Parade."

"Sure, let's roll back the years. I had just gone solo, and I was top of the bill at the Embassy. I was presented with a replica gold disc on Westward TV; I had an agent and a record deal, then it went tits up."

"Just to remind you that this goes out before the watershed."

"Oh shit, yeah. Anyway, as I was saying, I didn't know it then, but I was about to take another downhill dip on the rock and roll rollercoaster."

"And I think it's about time for some music. How about the follow up to 'Subs' Bench'?"

"I remember. 'Don't Call Us, We'll Call You'. Great song, should have been a hit if it wasn't for being dumped by the label."

"So here it is, folks – Shane Meredith and 'Don't Call Us'!"

***

The sad truth was that while Shane Meredith did hit the number-one spot in Plymouth, it was during a cold January when money was tight and he only sold two hundred copies before he was displaced by his rival, grammar-schoolboy Chris Richards with his group The Scimitars.

The label who dumped him was a tiny operation called Stonehouse Records and a disillusioned Shane decided that his only hope was to give up his steady job at Dingles and try his luck in the northern clubs. Now back to the interview…

***

"That was a great number, Shane. Will you be including it in your set, or will it be mainly new material?"

"My lips are sealed, Craig. I assume you are coming to the gig?"

"Wouldn't miss it for the world. Now, tell me about your time in the north?"

"Craig, those were real hard times, you know. I look back and call it the wilderness years."

"Was it hard to find work?"

"It was easier than back home. There were all these clubs up there, packed they were. I supported all the big names: Smokie, Peters and Lee, Black Lace, but I never headlined. And all the travelling up and down motorways in winter – rock and roll is a cruel mistress."

"You don't say. So how did you live?"

"It was tough. The gigs didn't pay well and so I had to play on sessions, bar work even. And the groupies, the paternity suits, it was a living nightmare, man."

"But then you met Janie."

"My lady, the love of my life. She turned it around."

"And you went behind what was then the Iron Curtain? That must have been an adventure!"

"It was crazy. I was so much bigger in Romania and Bulgaria than I was back here. Janie had this brainwave of getting me to wear a kilt and pretend to be Scottish – the punters lapped it up until the government decided to chuck us out."

"What was it, Shane – did they think that you represented the decadent West, drugs and free love?"

"Nah. It was the lyrics to one of the songs. It wasn't even one of my own, it was by Randy Newman. I never knew why it was such a huge underground hit in Bucharest, but it turned out they loved it because they thought it was laughing at the president."

"What was the song called?"

"'Short People'. And the president was a short geezer, so we had to hotfoot it."

"So why don't we relive those wild days! This is 'Short People', the Randy Newman version of Shane's eastern-bloc-busting hit!"

***

The relationship with Janie didn't survive the flight home from Romania. Shane slunk back to his parents and tried but failed to get his old job back. Dingles was by now part of the House of Fraser group and his previous employment in the old flagship store cut zero ice at interview. His long hair and dark glasses probably didn't help.

A brief spell as a porter introduced him to the world of hospital radio, and he soon wangled a regular slot on Thursday nights, playing a mixture of his old favourites and requests for Queen and ABBA, which he delivered through gritted teeth.

The broadcasting experience led him to try his luck in the States and he spent several years out there as an itinerant disc jockey on obscure radio stations, from Arkansas all the way up to Vermont.

He formed various short-lived relationships along the way, briefly found God in Georgia, lost him in Louisiana, and then he made the momentous and emotional decision to come home. A lot of his fellow singer-songwriters had enjoyed UK comebacks in the twenty-first century, so perhaps this was his time.

"If Cat Stevens can land the Pyramid Stage, then why not Shane Meredith?" he told himself after an impromptu gig at a country fair in Rhode Island.

So, here he is, back where it all started, being interviewed by Craig Lagor at the very same hospital radio station where he had cut his broadcasting teeth all those decades ago. Back to the interview.

***

"So, Shane. The comeback kid! You look great by the way, loving the new look."

"Yeah, I decided that I needed a new image, feel part of the scene, so I've gone for a retro Pet Shop Boys vibe."

"So that explains the short hair and the very smart suit."

"Indeed, it does. I used to work in tailoring back in the day, so I've always had an eye for clobber."

"Where was it you worked? John Collier?"

"The window to watch? Nah, Dingles. Much classier."

"So, Shane. The world tour. You are opening right here!"

"Yeah, the homecoming. I thought I owed it to the fans; they've never forgotten me, Craig. This one's for them."

"I'll be there, and we will be recording it for a special show later in the year. Ladies and gentlemen, it's been my honour and privilege to talk to the great Shane Meredith! And now over to Dirk Arnold at the sports desk."

***

The house lights dimmed, and then a super-smooth prerecorded voice invited the expectant audience to welcome to the stage the legendary superstar Shane Meredith.

The nursing home had issued toy tambourines to the residents, who shook them with glee as the great man slowly emerged onto the stage from a fog of dry ice.

"Good evening, Plymouth! It's great to be back! Let's see if you remember this one!"

He sang to a backing track, but the audience were clearly unfamiliar with the words, so Shane was met with deafening silence when he held out his mike for the crowd to sing the anthemic chorus of 'Stuck on the Subs' Bench of Love'.

"Come on, yeah, join in. *Stuck on the subs bench, give me some game time baby!*"

The crowd was getting restless.

"Play something we know!"

"Boo! This is rubbish. We want the Ukulele Man!"

"Play 'Roll out the Barrel'!"

"Or Queen or ABBA!"

Shane declined to be interviewed by Craig Lagor after the show and waited for the bus back to Crownhill, as he had done when he was at school.

But this time, instead of heading back to the loving arms of his mum and dad, he was bound for the cheap-as-chips Airbnb he'd rented for the week.

As he sat on the top deck of the bus and looked down at the lights of his hometown, he reflected that rock and roll was still a cruel mistress but that it was too late to escape her clutches. He was in it for life.

Shane Meredith will return. Oh yeah, baby.

He'd already got a great idea to challenge for the

Christmas number one: 'Hey, Repair Shop – Can You Mend a Broken Heart?'.

A Cornishman's Imagined Journey Home for the Final Christmas

I'd get the car ready the day before, check the oil and the tyre pressures, top up the screen wash.

The Christmas playlist had been lined up weeks ago. Kate Rusby, Cara Dillon, the McGarrigle Christmas hour, and 'That'll be Christmas' by Thea Gilmore, timed for the precise moment when I caught my first sight of the Coming-Home Trees.

I would glimpse them for the very last time through the rear-view mirror.

Absolutely no Chris Rea or Slade, and, God forbid, no room for Mariah on this valedictory parade.

At Dunheved Bridge, I'd feel the heart leap as I made my final crossing of the Tamar: 'One and All'.

I'm properly on my way now, the familiar signs warming the soul of the returning native – Polyphant, Tregadillet, Launceston, home to the great poet of the county, Charles Causley.

The du Maurier influence begins its beguiling descent

into the county as I pass Alturnan and its magnificent cathedral of the moors, a reproach to the tacky but iconic sign for Jamaica Inn.

Then further down, as the daylight fades over the moor, St Breward, and a last wave to the memory of Mary and Jenefer.

Blisland – now wouldn't that have made a great title for a novel, or a folk-rock album? Someone else will have to write it…

Garish lights at the huge service station; old Ronald McDonald illuminating the perpetual roadworks on the A30.

But none of the negative stuff mattered. I was on my way home. I was going to make it, surely.

I'd be in the bar by nine, enveloped in hugs. The singers would appear as I started my second pint, then I'd stumble to one of Betjeman's favourite churches as midnight mass was about to begin, with the Cornish folk song 'The Faraway Tale of the Sweet Nightingale' still ringing in my ears as I left the pub and headed towards the moss-encrusted lychgate, still wet from the afternoon rain.

Then, as the bells started to ring out to herald the infant birth, I'd amble back to my adjacent cottage, climb the stairs, and soon drift into a deep cocoa sleep with the window open, waking for the briefest moment on Christmas morning to glimpse the last of the Kernow moon as I took in my final breath of the sweetest air in Christendom.

A Close Encounter: John Tedesco Investigates

Carefully positioning himself behind one of the chubbiest of the columns in the chapel of St Nonna, Tedesco patiently awaited the appearance of the cheating couple.

As if on cue, the furtive duo crept into the little haven that was set aside for quiet prayer and Tedesco deftly switched on his phone to record their predictably banal dialogue.

The man said, "Are you feeling as guilty as I am?"

The woman said, "Yah, but it turns me on. I mean it *rarely, rarely* does."

Tedesco had to control himself from giggling. This was like listening to an audiobook version of something by Jackie Collins; although, after some reflection, Jilly Cooper would be more socially and geographically appropriate.

"Being here after evensong, with the place to ourselves," he said.

"Have you ever fantasised about…" she started to reply.

"What, here in the cathedral? On one of those old tombs?"

She, suddenly doubtful, said, "Yah. But now we've finally got the chance…"

"It doesn't feel right. In the house of God and so on."

"I know. Even though I don't believe anymore, it just feels a bit, you know, creepy. And it's bloody cold in here."

To Tedesco's intense relief – he certainly wasn't 'turned on' by the seediness of what he had just overheard – the couple slipped out of the building via the dean's door.

What he recorded wasn't of itself evidence of adultery, but it justified his client's suspicion.

He had been reluctant to accept the job. Diana Beaumaris had approached him at coffee after Sunday morning eucharist and had breathily invited him back to her magnificent apartment in the Cathedral Close, as she needed his advice on a matter of extreme delicacy.

After two large gin and tonics, she blurted out that she was convinced that her husband Gilo was having an affair with her best friend Gilly Frazer, who was a well-upholstered widow who owned an equally desirable dwelling which boasted spectacular views of the Tower.

She continued, "Now, if it was just about sex, I could live with it, as long as it didn't become public knowledge, in which case the humiliation would be ghastly. But I think it's more than that. I really think they might be getting serious."

John Tedesco kept his initial thoughts to himself and let her carry on.

He was in his late fifties and had never married or even lived with someone, although he had suffered from more than his fair share of unrequited love.

Perhaps this is how the upper classes roll? he speculated to himself.

Keep it discreet, don't give the servants any cause to gossip and don't, whatever you do, get serious. Or found out.

Diana Beaumaris interrupted his musings. She said, very firmly, "Mr Tedesco, you have listened so patiently. Would you take on my case? I just need to know if it's true. It goes without saying that I will pay double your usual hourly charge."

The agency could do with some well-paying clients. His business partner, Lynne, still carried out some corporate recruitment work from her new home in Bath, but as the spate of murders in the cathedral had, mercifully, dried up, he was becoming reliant on this kind of stuff – tailing errant husbands.

Although he found the work distasteful and completely unglamorous – why did adulterers, swingers, dogging enthusiasts and their ilk often turn out to be what Wodehouse described as 'horrendous specimens' – he couldn't afford to turn this one down.

It would be tricky though. The action, such as it might turn out to be, would be taking place on his refined doorstep. But beggars can't be choosers.

***

Once he had returned from the stakeout at the cathedral to his office in Minster Precincts, he listened to the recording and then dictated a report of what he had heard into his ancient Dictaphone.

It was 2023, but this was how he still chose to operate. When he had completed the task, he barked 'end of tape' into the machine, removed the audio cassette from the little handheld device and passed it to his PA, Sally Munks, with the instruction that this was urgent, adding his trademark reminder about the importance of client confidentiality.

Then he addressed his border terrier, who was trying to catch up with some sleep from the safety of his basket located under his master's desk.

"Come on, Barker. Your master needs some thinking time."

Passing Sally on his way out, he told her that they would be back within the hour. The detective and his canine pal, having survived the death-trap staircase which led from 4A Minster Precincts to the communal entrance of what Tedesco liked to refer to as a medieval office block, entered the outer Cathedral Close, where they greeted Jos Elsted, a friendly wine merchant who had just taken a lease of 4B.

Jos and Tedesco had discussed an unofficial merger of the two businesses. Tedesco was a wine buff and Jos had demonstrated potential as a detective in the recent case of the Turbulent Bishop.

"Perhaps it's time to talk to Jos again, now he's finally moved in? What do you reckon, Barker? 'Crime and Wine'. It has a certain ring to it, don't you think?"

Barker looked up as if to say, "You woke me up just for that?"

They continued their perambulation of the vast expanse of the cathedral grounds in companionable silence until they reached Tedesco's favourite 'mulling bench', which was mercifully free of tourists, snogging teenagers or more mature locals stopping to admire the view of the West Front.

Barker jumped up beside him for a well-earned stroke.

His master said, "This is when I miss Lynne, old pal. She would be so much better at confronting Lady Beaumaris with the evidence."

***

As a dog who believed in routine, Barker was very confused early that evening. Having been walked home and fed at the usual time, his boss was leaving him and going out again.

Tedesco showered and changed into his smart-casual attire – pressed chinos, Crew Company top-and-deck shoes – before heading back into the Close via the South Gate.

He and Barker lived in 17 St Budeaux Place, a bijou mews house situated just outside the Close but within the 'ancient liberty'.

His client, eager to find out what Tedesco had uncovered, had messaged him to 'pop round' at seven o'clock for an aperitif.

Feeling somewhat conspicuous as he climbed the steps leading to the front door of the Dalton Canonry, he hesitated a while before opting to try the doorbell rather than the terrifying pull.

After an agonising wait, which was probably only thirty seconds, the vast door was opened by a liveried butler who admitted him to an antechamber which came complete with a small table displaying copies of *The Field*, *Country Life* and *The Spectator*.

Having accepted the offer of a seat, he had just started to thumb through the pages of *Country Life* when his senses were assailed by the familiar scent of Lady Beaumaris's floral perfume.

She greeted him with a somewhat forced enthusiasm. "Mr Tedesco! Thank you *so* much for taking the time. You must be incredibly busy without Lynne to help you out."

Before the detective could respond, he found himself being swept into the magnificent drawing room where his client had summoned a servant who suddenly appeared with a fully laden drinks trolley.

This slightly wrongfooted him – he had assumed that nowadays such contraptions were reserved for the use of amateur theatre companies performing Alan Aykbourn farces – or was her ladyship demonstrating a previously well-concealed talent for irony?

He followed his client's lead in choosing a gin and tonic – somewhat heavy on the gin – and once the waiter had trundled off, Diana Beaumaris slid further up the chaise longue, patting the side that she had vacated.

"Please, don't be shy," she said.

Tedesco was – is – shy. Pathologically so, his sister would say. The introvert's introvert.

He moved awkwardly towards the no doubt priceless item of furniture, shakily placing his drink on the table opposite and then he sat down awkwardly next to his client, looking for the world as if he would rather have a major artery removed without anaesthetic.

Lady Beaumaris got to the point. She said, "So, Mr Tedesco. I've been beside myself with excitement all day. What have you got for me?"

Trying and failing to suppress a blush, the master sleuth handed her ladyship a copy of the transcript of the overheard conversation in the chapel.

Affixing her reading glasses with what Tedesco would later describe to his friend Jos as a ridiculously theatrical flourish, her ladyship read the document carefully and then handed it back.

"Well done, Mr Tedesco! Or can I call you John?" she whispered seductively. "Your reputation is well deserved," she added, "but are you quite sure that Gilly and Giles didn't see you?"

"Yes, Lady Beaumaris," he replied with an emphasis designed to negate her attempt at a more intimate relationship.

It failed.

"John," she whispered again, almost sexily, sidling ever closer to him, "what will you do with this? It's clear evidence, isn't it?"

"Er, no, not of adultery per se," he responded.

Diana Beaumaris grimaced at the sound of the 'A' word, and at Tedesco's legalistic tone.

He continued. "It is evidence of a close friendship, and of an intention to at least contemplate the act, but that is all it is."

"So," her ladyship replied, "will you be tailing them until, I don't know, they check into some awful Travel Inn or whatever they call themselves?"

Resisting the pedantic temptation to point out they would be checking in to either a Travelodge or a Premier Inn, Tedesco responded by reminding his client that he acted upon her instructions.

She may choose to terminate his retainer now and confront her husband with what he had uncovered, or she might instruct him to continue to investigate with the aim of seeking incontrovertible evidence.

She slid even closer to him and said, breathily, "John, my husband is up in town tonight. You have been such a star. Why don't we continue to discuss this over supper?"

Before he could make his excuses – he already had a date with Barker and a Charlie Bigham meal for one – the butler, footman or whatever he was silently appeared as if by magic. The servant spoke. "Excuse me, madam, but I thought I should let you know that Sir Giles has just arrived."

Once the factotum had duly 'factoted' himself back to the servants' quarters or wherever, her ladyship placed her hand on Tedesco's thigh.

"We will have to continue our little chat some other time, I fear. I simply can't let Gilo see us together; he is so jealous."

"Well, I can assure him that he has nothing to be jealous of," said an alarmed Tedesco, before adding that it would be unwise for Sir Giles to get wind of his investigation.

She, somewhat thrown by the news of her husband's arrival, said, "Look, I am so sorry, John, but if you head out through the door you entered and turn right there is a fire escape. It takes you to the tradesman's door and then you can slip into the Close unseen."

The detective didn't delay, and managed, not without difficulty, to negotiate the iron spiral stairs that led outside. He resolved to make an extra charge for danger money.

***

"Darling, why didn't you ring, or at least send me one of those ghastly text messages?" asked Lady Beaumaris.

"I wanted to surprise you," said her husband. "I was able to get out of the trustees meeting early, and I didn't fancy hanging around in town, so I jumped on the 5:21pm."

"Well, it is a surprise, Gilo. You should have let me know so that I could have warned the kitchen that there would be two for supper."

"Yes, sorry about that," said Sir Giles, noticing the two gin tumblers.

He added, heavily, "But I see that you have had company, darling one."

Straight off the bat, Diana Beaumaris said that Gilly Frazer had popped by for a girl's gossip.

Sir Giles knew that this was a lie as he'd been with Gilly all afternoon. In a Holiday Inn, as it transpired.

And as he arrived home, he had noticed a male silhouette making a less-than-graceful exit down the fire escape.

In the meantime, Tedesco had arrived back at St Budeaux Place and made his peace with Barker.

After wolfing down his Bigham's lasagne on a tray while watching *Channel Four News* on catch-up, he retreated to his den with a glass of Jos Elsted's latest recommendation: a plummy South African red in the Bordeaux style, slightly heavy on the cabernet franc.

He fussed and riffled among the sleeves of his extensive vinyl collection in search of a track that would match his current investigation and the farcical turn it had just taken.

"The very thing, Barker! You will remember this one!"

He gently opened the gatefold sleeve, reread the lyric sheet, then extracted the precious waxing contained therein, before giving it a loving polish with his microfibre cleaning brush as if it was an exhibit in a museum.

Then he lowered the album onto the turntable with ceremonial care, and placed the needle on side two, track one.

The touching, haunting, grammatically correct 'You Well-Meaning Brought Me Here', his favourite Ralph McTell song.

***

After a surprisingly untroubled sleep, bearing in mind his

ordeal of the previous evening, Tedesco led Barker through the Close on their familiar, glorious walk to work.

Their progress was, as usual, delayed by various conversations. Canon Wilfred Drake greeted them both as he headed back home across Cathedral Green after early morning communion, legendary local reporter Julie Stringer stopped to ask how Lynne was doing in Bath and then Lady Derrington, the unofficial president of the Barker Appreciation Society, fell into step with them as she headed to a meeting of Cathedral Chapter.

So, it came as something of a shock to Tedesco, after such a predictably pleasant start to his day, to arrive at 4A St Budeaux Place to be greeted by a starstruck Sally, his excitable PA.

She said, lightly, "Mr T! You are here!"

He said, sarcastically, "Where else would I be on a weekday morning, Sally, on a manned mission to Mars? On the morning TV sofa with Lorraine Kelly?"

"Your master is so funny sometimes, isn't he, Barker?"

No comment, said Barker's expression.

"Anyway, you will never guess who our latest client is going to be?" Sally asked her boss.

Tedesco looked at his watch. "Spit it out. Elton John, perhaps? The weather presenter from *BBC Searchlight*?"

"No! It's Sir Giles Beaumaris!"

"Sally, I really hope that you haven't made an appointment for him. Oh God, you have. When is he coming?"

"He should be here any minute. He wants to see you urgently before he goes up to London."

"OK. Sally, emergency black coffee now, please. I will be in the interview room."

Barker conked out under his human friend's desk while the detective headed for the little room set aside for quiet research, and for seeing clients of the firm.

Tedesco extracted a blue counsel's notebook from the desk drawer and produced his fountain pen from his suit pocket.

His instinctive reaction, apart from one of annoyance at Sally for making an appointment with a potential new client without reference to him, was that this was going to be a very short meeting. He would just tell Sir Giles that he had an unspecified conflict of interest which precluded him from taking on his case.

On further consideration though, perhaps he ought to hear what Sir Giles had to say.

He may be consulting him on something entirely unrelated to his alleged affair, or he may be acting on behalf of one of his many charitable connections.

Sally knocked on the door and introduced Sir Giles with a mixture of effusiveness and obsequiousness.

The aristocrat was dressed for the City in a blue chalk stripe suit, immaculately ironed white double-cuffed shirt matched with what Tedesco assumed was the tie of his old school or maybe his livery company and highly polished brogues.

"I will come to the point, Mr Tedesco. I seek your advice on a pressing issue of the utmost delicacy. You have been highly recommended by several contacts of mine, principally Sir Vere Alston."

Sir Vere was the previous member of parliament for the Rhyminster constituency and was someone whom Tedesco held in considerable esteem.

The detective gestured for Sir Giles to continue.

"Mr Tedesco, I expect we are both of about the same vintage? So, you may remember the Milk Tray Man?"

"Yes, of course. He was a mysterious chap dressed in black who seemed at first blush to be a James Bond secret-agent figure but was in fact going to extreme lengths to deliver boxes of mass-produced chocolates to impossibly glamourous women."

"So, you are no doubt wondering," said Sir Giles, "why is this chap sitting opposite me chuntering on about the Milk Tray Man?"

Tedesco gave a shy smile. "I wouldn't put it as crudely as that, and you hear all manner of strange things in this job. But do tell me what this has to do with your approach to us. How can I help?"

Sir Giles leaned forward. "I saw him. Last night."

"Who did you see, Sir Giles?"

"The Milk Tray Man, of course."

"Er. And when and where did you see him?"

"At home last night. The Dalton Canonry. He was escaping down the fire exit. The blackguard didn't see me, but I saw him. He'd been ravishing my wife in the drawing room."

At this point, there was a somewhat apologetic knock on the door. Tedesco would normally have been extremely irritated to be interrupted by Sally when interviewing clients, but this time he could have hugged her. Or so at first he thought.

Sally, entering the room, said, "I'm so sorry, Mr Tedesco, but Lady Beaumaris is here."

Her ladyship didn't wait to be invited in, nor to speak. "Giles! What on earth are you doing here?"

"I could ask you the same question, darling."

"And John!" she said as she pointed an immaculately varnished fingernail at him. "You are supposed to be acting for me!"

The gentle detective stood up. And then he said, "If we can just calm down and look at the facts. This agency has been instructed by you, Lady Beaumaris," he continued, with considerable patience. "My secretary, without my knowledge, had arranged for your husband to see me at very short notice. I was going to explain to him that I had identified a conflict of interest which would prevent me from acting on his behalf, but upon reflection, I decided that I would afford Sir Giles the opportunity to explain what he was consulting me about, as it may not have been related to your matter. He may have been approaching me on behalf of others."

Her ladyship glared at both of them and then she addressed Tedesco. "John, I am disappointed, but I will give you the benefit of the doubt. It sounds as if you were acting professionally, but you might want to train that ditsy assistant of yours to think before she engages her brain."

Tedesco sprang to Sally's defence, knowing full well that her ear would be pressed to the wall.

"Giles," her ladyship continued, the wind firmly in her sails, "I know all about your affair with Gilly and this is why I asked John to investigate. I have all the proof I need, so I suggest you stay at your club until you hear from my lawyers. I want a divorce.

"John," her ladyship went on in similar vein, "get Daisy Daydream to send me your account."

Tedesco suppressed a chuckle. Sally had been given many nicknames over the years, but this was a new one.

"Now, look here, Diana," boomed Sir Giles. "You might as well know. I came to see Tedesco about the Milk Tray Man."

"Giles, are you going raving mad?"

"No. I saw him last night, shinning down the fire escape."

'Shinning' is a bit of an exaggeration, thought Tedesco. *'Descending uncertainly' might be a more accurate description.*

Lady Beaumaris burst out laughing. "It wasn't the Milk Tray Man. It was John Tedesco!"

ABOUT THE AUTHOR

After a long career in the law, most of it spent in private practice in Winchester, Radu retired from full-time legal work in 2019 to concentrate on his writing.

To date, he has successfully published three books in the John Tedesco Cathedral Murder series, with 2023's *The Turbulent Bishop* following hot on the heels of *The Cage*, which was described as having shades of Anthony Trollope's Barchester novels by *The Law Society Gazette* and *Leap of Faith*.

Radu spent his formative years in Devon and Hampshire and now he lives in Salisbury with Lucinda, where he divides his time between creating the Tedesco series and volunteering at the cathedral as a guide and steward.

He is currently working on the next Tedesco mystery.

This book is printed on paper from sustainable sources managed under the Forest Stewardship Council (FSC) scheme.

It has been printed in the UK to reduce transportation miles and their impact upon the environment.

For every new title that Troubador publishes, we plant a tree to offset CO_2, partnering with the More Trees scheme.

MORE TREES
LET'S PLANT A BILLION TREES

For more about how Troubador offsets its environmental impact, see www.troubador.co.uk/sustainability-and-community